Just a Piece of Red String

Antebellum Voodoo and Vengeance

by

Dr. Thomas S. Smith, Sr.

Dedicated to my father,
James Thomas Smith,
a disabled
veteran of the Pacific Theater
in World War II
and recipient of four bronze stars,
and my mother,
Bessie Mildred Smith,
his loving wife.

ACKNOWLEDGEMENTS

Special Thanks

Shirley Tassin

Christopher Flanders

Grace M. S. McKittrick MacNeil

and my

Smith Family

"The past is a foreign country:
they do things differently there."—L. P. Hartley

Just a Piece of Red String:

Antebellum Voodoo and Vengeance

Natchez, Mississippi, 1849

"And the apostles said unto the Lord, 'Increase our faith.' And the Lord said, 'If ye had faith as a grain of mustard seed, ye might say unto this sycamine tree, Be thou plucked up by the root, and be thou planted in the sea, and it should obey yew.'" The wrinkled, feeble, old woman with the scratchy voice carefully placed the old piece of faded red string she used as a bookmark into her old Bible and slowly closed it. Elnora Dundee, in a bright yellow dress, looked down at the children seated in front of her old rocking chair, talking about what she had just read to them and pointing out to a tree.

"Yew, younguns, see that sycamine there in the yard, neer the road. If yew had faith to match the size of the wee seed of the mustard plant, then yew could work a wonder and uproot the sycamine and chunk it into the Mississippi River, and it'd wash rat on down to the Gulf. Yew younguns listen to this heer old woman, her Bible readin'. Do yew heer?"

Pausing for a moment, old Elnora looked down and around at the little faces of the children there. The boys and girl shook their heads up and down and dutifully responded, "Yes, ma'am" or "Yes, Grandma." Stelcie Dundee, youngest of the group, grinned a front-tooth-missing grin at her Grandma Dundee. Her older brother, Sawyer, was still pondering the sycamine bush when Grandma called his name.

"Sawyer Dundee."

Sawyer quickly turned his face around and up to her.

"Yew puzzled, boy. Yew must have faith."

Beside Sawyer was a small black boy, son of a slave the Dundees owned. The boy's father worked in the sawmill with his master, Jeremiah Dundee. The smaller boy's name was Gabriel.

Next to Gabriel was Solomon Witcher. Solomon and Sawyer had been born on the same day. Solomon was a cousin of Stelcie and Sawyer and had come to live with the Dundees when his father went off to the Mexican War.

"Yew tryin' to figer out what this heer old woman be saying about that sycamine, ain't yew, Solomon Witcher?" The old woman took a sip from her cup of mint-flavored water.

"Yes ma'am, Grandma Dundee."

"It'll be easy for yew, little Witcher. Jist keep eyein' that sycamine ever time yew pass by it. It'll be easy for yew. It'll strike yew one day. Have faith. Use what the good Lord above give yew, boy. Use what yew got for the Lord!"

Stelcie and Gabriel and Sawyer, looking bewildered, stared at Solomon. And ten-year-old Solomon stared first at Grandma Dundee and then at the sycamine bush, wondering. It was a small moment frozen in time. It was a mustard seed for things to come.

Natchez, Mississippi, 1859

"That sycamine tree is sweltering just like me, Mama, I do declare it's so hot so early this summer," said Stelcie to Laura Dundee. The mother and daughter sat on the front porch of the Dundee home, trying to catch any little breeze that wafted onto unenclosed porch.

"Yes, Stelcie, it's hot today. It's only early afternoon, too. I hope yore Daddy stays in the shade over at the sawmill. He works too hard. Just like yore grandpappy did. Yew know yore grandpappy just up and died one hot summer afternoon at that sawmill. Yore daddy's gonna do the same thing. I jist know it. I jist fear it."

"I know, Mama. Maybe Daddy'll slow down when the boys git back and go to work agin. I hope it's not so hot tomorrow afternoon when we go meet 'em at the steamboat landing. There ain't hardly no trees down there. We'll have to wear our broad-brimmed hats, won't we, Mama? I have that new yellow dress for visiting Daddy bought me for my sixteenth birthday. The other dress, the red one, is for the party at the Surgets."

"Isn't it nice, dear, that the Surgets are putting on a party, a birthday party, at Clifton for yew and Miriam. She's a nice girl. I surely wish I had a niece as sweet as Miriam. I jist wish I had a niece or more nephews than only poor Solomon Witcher. It's a shame that almost all of yore daddy's people died in that yellow fever epidemic years ago in northern Mississippi. That's why he came here to Natchez, to make a new start."

"But what about Solomon's family, Mama? Some of them survived, didn't they?"

"Yes, dear. Yore right."

"Solomon's mother was Daddy's youngest sister. Right, Mama?"

"Yes, dear. But she died when birthing Solomon. Then the fever hit a few months later. The only ones who took the fever and lived were baby Solomon and his daddy. They were inseparable for a time. I supposed that Cain mourned so much for yore Aunt Sarah and all his other children that he had to keep a hold on little Solomon. They even came to live with us for a time before yew were born."

"But, Mama, Uncle Cain I remember," said Stelcie.

"Yew were young when he came by on his way to the Mexican War. When he left Solomon with Grandma Dundee and us. And Grandma brought him up. She always said he was something special. Something really—"

"Was Uncle Cain killed in the war?" interrupted Stelcie.

"We never got word. We don't rightly know. He was reported missing. But his body was never found. No official word of his death came to us. We had hoped that he would turn up one day. He had hard times in general, but fortune always smiled on him as an individual. I reckon he was a good man, especially if your Aunt Sarah married him. I don't rightly know him."

"Y'all had hoped he would come back from the war? But he was probably killed, or he would've been back," said Stelcie.

"We hoped and prayed he'd be back for Solomon's sake. But that was years ago," replied Laura Dundee. "A long time ago."

"Tomorrow's not too long from now, Mama. I can't wait to see Saw and Solomon. I have a lot to tell 'em. I'll introduce 'em to Miriam and—"

"We all have much to talk about, and they'll tell us the feelin's of the Yankees up there where they went to school about the slavery issue and our states' rights belief. Yore daddy will want to hear about that."

10

"Politics! Politics! That and slavery! All them Yankees! What don't they leave us be?"

"Well, dear Stelcie, it's menfolk talk. Don't get yoreself flustered. It won't amount to nothing no way. Drink yore tea, dear."

"It's simply not fair," mused Stelcie in a low voice.

Mother and daughter, now feeling a more vigorous wind, sat quietly on the porch and gazed outward at the road about a hundred yards away. They heard the noises of a wagon creaking and voices from its passengers. When the wagon appeared, they saw it was driven by an old slave they knew by the name of Enoch. He was bent over, and his gray hair and beard could be seen, even though he had on a hat, itself old. The wagon was loaded with several wooden crates and large sacks and four slave boys who were ten to twelve years of age. The boys were laughing and shouting now. It must have been that Enoch had seen the Dundees on the porch watching the wagon because he turned quickly to the loud boys and said in a firm but not too loud voice, "Hesh up, boys, hesh." The four boys obediently and abruptly ended their laughing and yelling. He hollered out a greeting to the Dundee women. They shouted back and waved in a friendly manner to old Enoch. The mule plodded slowly but surely onward.

As Stelcie and her mother watched the wagon disappear from sight and heard the laughter and voices of the slave boys once more, Laura Dundee looked at the daughter and then at the road where the wagon had been and mused, "Fairness has nothing to do with it."

The humidity was high on this June afternoon, and a few gray clouds were floating in, rather lazily it seemed. The cooling wind had died down for the last few minutes. Stelcie and Mrs. Dundee now felt a light stirring of the air and then a gentle breeze.

"It might rain before night," said Mrs. Dundee, as she looked upward at the summer sky. "Things might cool off."

"Mama, is our house big enough for all of us now—with Sawyer and Solomon returning home, I mean?" asked Stelcie.

"Yes, shore it is, why do yew ask somethin' like that?"

"Well, Mama, I was just thinkin' about Miriam and the Surgets and their Clifton and all the other plantation homes around here. Our house is not nothing like those. And Daddy's in the sawmill business and owns some land besides our homestead here. And he owns only a few nigger slaves," Stelcie said.

"Now Stelcie, yew know yore daddy. He don't want one of them big mansions, as he calls them. He says that's fine and dandy for anybody that wants one and has one. But he says he don't need one. I think so, too. We're fine. Yew remember that yore Daddy says, 'It don't matter how many rooms yew have in yore house, yew can only sleep in the one bed.' Our house is big compared with what most folks have. Most other folks might call what we have a mansion. Think about our house and homestead. We built on rooms as we needed them. Yew and the boys all have yore separate rooms upstairs. The house help has a little room off the kitchen. And we have the colored houses out back by the barn. Besides that, yew know yore daddy don't care 'bout owning too many slaves. He don't like the idea of owning another person. He and I have talked about owning slaves many times. There is much yew don't know 'bout yore daddy's thinking about the whole issue of slavery. Why, yew don't know about Beulah . . . , oh, that's somethin' we will talk 'bout another time in the future when yew are all growed up. I won't say nothin' more right now."

"But, Mama, we don't have the chandeliers and mirrors an—"

"Now yew hush up, little girl! We don't need such fancy stuff. We're just plain working folks who have a big house and a good life because of yore daddy's hard work. We don't need no fancy Greek columns for this porch. Why, yore Grandma Dundee sat on this very porch and read to yew children from her Bible and taught yew values. It was good enough for her, and it's good enough for me and yew! Child, I don't rightly know what's got into yore mind! Now hush up yore nonsense!"

"Yes, ma'am, Mama. I was just saying what—"

"Let's talk about something else. Won't yew be glad to see Sawyer and Solomon?"

"Yes, ma'am. It'll be nice to have 'em back. Jist like old times around here."

"Remember all of yew have grown up, Stelcie. Why just look at yew. And the boys. Well, they're young men now," said Mrs. Dundee.

"I remember, Mama. I remember when we were little. Grandma Dundee, on the porch, the sycamine bush. We played around that sycamine bush, and Solomon would make up scary stories about his pulling up the sycamine with its roots and chuc

king it into the river and its coming back to life as an evil creature with seven heads. But Solomon would always save us at the end," related Stelcie. "Grandma Dundee always told him he was special. Why, Mama?"

"Don't ask me, Stelcie," answered Mrs. Dundee. "Maybe it was because he survived the illness when all his brothers and sisters perished. Maybe it was because his daddy left him with her, and us, when he went off to the Mexican War and didn't come back. Maybe she knew he needed more love, a special feeling of belonging, something. Grandma Dundee had her ways, but she knew how to love all of us. Yew didn't feel slighted, did yew?"

"Not, not really. I know she loved me. Saw knew she loved him. But we, we both realized that Grandma seemed to embrace

Solomon, to aim her Bible readings at him, to spiritualize at him more than us. We jist supposed he needed more from her," replied Stelcie.

"I declare, Stelcie Dundee, yew are beginin' to sound more and more like an adult every day."

"Why, thank yew, Mama."

The breeze quickened, and both noticed more gray clouds in the distant sky.

"Yew and Daddy have treated Solomon jist like one of us, yore own children. Y'all loved him and cared for him jist as yew did for us. Daddy's sent him off to school with Saw. Not that I ponder on it, Mama; I think yew let Solomon off easy many times from his boyish mischief. He could talk himself out of trouble with yew and sometimes even Grandma. And yew know I couldn't never stay angry at him for long. He could sweet talk me every time."

"Me, too, Stelcie. I jist could not stay mad at that boy. The way he grinned up at me. And the impish twinkle in his eyes. I declare," added Mrs. Dundee. "I am anxious to see them boys. I'm happy they've finished their schooling. It'll be easier on Jeremiah now with Sawyer and Solomon back."

Lightning flashed in the distance, and a crack of thunder broke from the sky. Heavy, dark clouds were massing in the distance.

"Mercy sakes!" exclaimed a startled Mrs. Dundee. The wind gusted. "It looks like it blowing up a storm over yonder. Let's go inside and look at yore party dress. I might stitch on that lace yet."

"I'll get yore tea glass, Mama."

"Beulah. Beulah," called out Mrs. Dundee as she went through the door.

"Yes, Missus. I be here."

Beulah, the house help, was a slave in her late forties who was jolly, overweight, and outgoing in personality. She was only five feet in height. She always smiled a broad, toothy, genial smile that made everybody like her.

"Please fetch Stelcie's party dress for us, Beulah. And that length of lace I showed yew yesterday. Meet us in Stelcie's room, heah."

"Yes, Missus. Oh, Miss Stelcie, yew gonna be the prettiest young miss at that party over to da Clifton. Yew watch that yew be turning too many gentlemen's heads. Yew be marrying age," teased Beulah as she followed Mrs. Dundee and Stelcie up the staircase.

There was another clap of thunder, and heavy raindrops now pelted the Dundee homestead. The rain continued for several hours in intervals of light and heavy. It stopped after one extremely heavy downpour.

It was still light, but just barely so, when a wagon of field hands and hired workers turned off the main road onto the lesser road to the Dundee house. Alongside of the wagon was a horse and rider. Jeremiah Dundee rode past the house to the stable and barn. He was talking to the slaves and other workers, particularly the wagon driver.

As Jeremiah dismounted, he closed his conversation with, "Thanks for the hep at the mill. We put our rainy afternoon to good use. We needed to get that lumber loaded for delivery tomorrow." He paused, looked back at the house and then at the slave cabins, and asked as the slaves were getting down from the wagon, "Was that roof fixed on that last cabin theah?"

One slave who took the reins of Mr. Dundee's horse nodded and replied, "Yes, Massa Dundee. I's patched that leak hole dis mornin' afore the rains start. It don't leak no more."

Jeremiah looked at the driver of the wagon and said, "Why don't yew take the wagon and drive these others to the junction?"

"Yas, sur. I be glads to do dat. I's git rat back heah lickety-split," said the driver, smiling.

"Good. Good. Thank y'all fer the good work today!" He turned from the wagon as it moved away, and he started toward the house and suddenly turned again and hollered, "Cole. Cole."

"Yes, Massa?"

"Show me that new baby yew and Beth have. I ain't seen 'im. How old is he?" said Mr. Dundee.

"He be two days, Massa."

They walked toward the middle cabin side by side.

"Beth ain't ailin', is she?"

"No, sur."

At the porch of the small gray cabin, Cole bounced up the step ahead of Mr. Dundee and opened the door quickly and in an excited voice said, "Beth. Beth. Be quick! Massa Dundee be here to see the man-child."

Jeremiah Dundee was at the doorway and stood there momentarily. Cole had picked up one of the three old chairs and put it down by Dundee for him to sit.

"Hello, Beth."

"Massa Dundee, sits down, please," said Beth with a delighted smile on her face.

"Jist for a time," said Dundee as he sat. "I came to see the little one."

Beth, still grinning proudly because of her new baby and because Master Dundee had come, reached down into a new wooden cradle and picked up her child. She advanced to where Dundee sat. "Here, see, Massa. His name be Benjamin."

"Benjamin, eh? A fine Bible name," Dundee said as he reached out his rough hands to touch the baby's small hand. Benjamin's little fingers instinctively grabbed Dundee's index finger and tugged. "Oh, and a strong grip on this little one! He'll be working by his daddy in no time."

Cole grinned.

"I must git up to the house now," stated Mr. Dundee as he rose from the old chair. "Yew two take good care of this baby." He turned and paused at the door, looked directly in the eyes of the two slave parents, and said, "In his lifetime, he will be a free man."

"Yes, Massa Dundee," said Beth and Cole smiling.

"Beth, did Mrs. Dundee git out heah today?"

"Yes, sur. She brung me birthing presents. The Missus give me this heah new kettle and this heah bolt of calico cloth and some more vegetables from de house," replied Beth. "An' she sended Beulah out with some supper vittles for us'n."

"Good." Dundee turned to go.

"Thank yew, Massa Dundee, thank yew, sur," said Cole.

"Yus, Massa," Beth added.

"See yew tomorrow morning," Mr. Dundee said as he strode out the cabin door, smiling.

Cole grinned as well and said to his wife, "Massa Dundee beens gud to us'n, to all their colored folks. I's wonders wat he mean remarking 'bout dis baby bein' a free man befores he leave dis world for de next." They looked at the baby in Beth's arm and smiled.

17

Mr. Dundee opened the kitchen back door and walked in, greeting Beulah as he did.

"Massa Dundee, yew be hungry, sur?" asked Beulah, grinning broadly.

"Why, yes, Beulah, I am. What did yew and Mrs. Dundee cook up for me this evening?"

"It be me and Miss Stelcie that done cooked tonight, Massa. We cooked up yore favorite, roast beef with rice and gravy and all the fixin's yew likes," replied Beulah.

"It sounds mighty good. I'll be back to eat here in the kitchen in a bit. Hep my plate for me, will yew?"

"Shore thing, Massa Dundee," returned Beulah with her usual pearly grin.

Mr. Dundee went out of the kitchen, through the dining room, and into the front room by the staircase. He called out, "Laura. Laura. Stelcie. Either of yew womenfolk up theah?"

"Yes, Daddy. Mama and I are up heah. We'll be down in a minute," came Stelcie's voice from the second floor.

Mr. Dundee turned and walked back to and through the kitchen, rolling up the sleeves of his work shirt as he went. "I'm going to warsh off some of this dirt and sawdust, Beulah. I'll be back in a twitch."

"Yus, sur."

Mr. Dundee was just beginning to eat his supper when Stelcie and Mrs. Dundee came in, jabbering away like a couple of magpies in the spring. Each went over to Mr. Dundee and kissed him on the cheek.

"The boys are coming in tomorrow, right?" asked Mr. Dundee.

18

"That's right, Daddy."

"Yes, Jeremiah. Sawyer's last letter said they'd be booked on the steamboat coming from Memphis. It's scheduled to be in by mid-afternoon," said Mrs. Dundee.

"It's two years since they were home. I wonder if they have changed much," Dundee reflected aloud.

"I'm sure they have, Daddy."

"Oh, they're handsome young men now. And educated," added Mrs. Dundee.

"That Sawyer's smarter than yew now, Daddy," teased Stelcie.

Beulah's smile faded as she was pouring Jeremiah more tea, and she said, "Now keep dat tongue of yorn still, Miss Stelcie! Them boys ain't no smarter than Massa Dundee. They jist be younger."

"Why, thank yew, Beulah."

"Dey be even more handsomer, though, I 'pose," added Beulah.

"Think so, Beulah?" asked Mr. Dundee, giving her a quizzical look.

"Yus, sur. Dat Saw will still have them piercing eyes, and dat Solomon still be a charmer. He could always talks me out of another biscuit or cookie," stated Beulah.

"Yes," said Mrs. Dundee, "they're young men now, but they'll still be themselves."

"It's getting late. I need some sleep. I'll be out early in the morning. Come on, Laura. Tell everyone good night."

"Yes, dear."

19

"Beulah," said Mr. Dundee, "remind Gabriel that I want him to go with the ladies to meet the boys at the landing under the hill tomorrow. He's to direct the boys by the mill as soon as the steamboat's in and their baggage is loaded on the wagon."

"Yes, Massa Dundee. I be atellin' him at furst light. Night, sur."

After the mid-day meal, Gabriel brought the wagon near the back door, got down from the driver's seat, and knocked on the open door.

"Beulah woman? Beulah woman? Is yew dere?" he called

"Shore be, Gabriel. What yew think? I works here all de times," replied Beulah. "Comes in."

Gabriel slowly walked into the kitchen and said, "It be the time that I wuz to hab de wagon and team bes ready. The horses be out dere readys to go."

"Missus Dundee and Stelcie be rat down from upstairs. Jist wait here. They's not be long. They's itching to gits to the landin' to see dem young mens agin," Beulah said rapidly while finishing the washing of the pots from the morning cooking.

"I sits here?" inquired Gabriel, pointing to a chair at the end of a medium-sized oak table.

As he was about to be seated, Beulah almost shouted, "No. Not dere. Dat be the Massa's place when he eats in the kitchen. I don't allows nobody 'cept him to sits dere. Yew sits over dere in dat chair." Beulah pointed to an older, worn chair, not next to the table.

But Gabriel did not have the opportunity to sit because as he strolled over to the chair, Stelcie burst into the kitchen exclaiming, "It's time for us to go, Beulah! Is Gabriel here?" She was wearing a bright yellow, full-skirted dress, clutching a lace handkerchief and a

20

broad-brimmed hat of the same shade as her dress. Before Beulah could answer, Stelcie saw him and exclaimed, "Oh, good. Yore here! I'll tell Mama." She turned abruptly and left the kitchen, leaving Beulah and Gabriel open-mouthed and then smiling.

Gabriel was the first to speak. "I be wondering about Sawyer and Solomon."

"What yew in wonderment 'bout, boy. All of us'n knowed dey be changed and different when dey be back from schoolin' up north. Dey be like yew, growed into manhood for shore by now," said Beulah.

"How much changed, Beulah woman? Massa Solomon he was . . . was—"

"Don't yew speak too much, boy! Massa Solomon was actin' peculiar the last time he—," Beulah ended her words abruptly as Mrs. Dundee and Stelcie came to the doorway.

"Gabriel. We're ready," stated Mrs. Dundee. She wore a dress and hat similar to Stelcie's but in an off-white color. Gabriel led the way out of the door and to the wagon.

He helped the ladies up on the seat and then climbed up on the wagon and stood behind them to drive. Behind the wagon he had tied two saddled horses, an Appaloosa stallion, which was Sawyer's, and an ash-black one, which was Solomon's.

"I's gots Country Boy and Midnight like Massa Dundee said," stated Gabriel as he made a clicking sound for the team to start pulling.

"I see," said Mrs. Dundee. "The boys'll be glad yew brought them along."

The wagon went at a steady brisk pace for fifteen minutes, passing several large plantation homes along the road into Natchez.

"Mama," said Stelcie, "why don't we have a carriage like the Surgets and the other fine families around here?"

"Yew know what yore daddy'd say to that question," replied Mrs. Dundee.

"That's fine for anybody else who wants one, but not for the Dundees, plain working folks," said Stelcie, glibly and mechanically.

They passed several smaller houses and entered Natchez. Now houses lined the road and intersecting streets. Stelcie chattered away, pointing here and there.

On their left appeared Rosalie, a beautiful, two-story home with four white columns on the front. The columns ran the height of the two floors, supporting a triangular area under the roof. A beautiful circular window centered itself in the white triangle. Red-orange brick with eight large block-shuttered windows, four on a floor, with white double-doors in the window presented a stately elegance. The tops of chimneys could be seen peeking from the rooftop edges on each side. Porches were on each level.

"Rosalie's a beautiful home, isn't it, Mama?" asked Stelcie in a dreamy manner.

"Yes, dear, it is. The side facing the river is lovely, too, with its larger porches and additional columns. But poor Peter Little died about two years ago. And Eliza. Just three years before, of the fever. He was never the same after her passing."

"The Wilsons are nice, though," injected Stelcie.

"Yes, Stelcie, we'll see them at the party," replied Mrs.Dundee.

"The party'll be just grand, Mama. I'm so looking forward to it."

In a few minutes they turned onto Silver Street that led to Natchez-Under-the-Hill and the steamboat landing. The dirt road was busy with wagons and riders on horses. The downward incline of the road was gradual, and the street itself was lined on the bluff side with mercantile stores. Farther down where the road leveled off, stores and buildings were on both sides for a little distance. The bluffs rose between 150 and 200 feet above the wooden buildings. Several of these structures were two stories in height. Some of the two-story structures had porches at the second floor. One had a wrought-iron railing. Mules were standing before half-loaded wagons scattered here and there in front of stores. Men, black and white, sweated in the hot sun, loading and unloading boxes and sacks of goods. Everyone was busy. One large sign dominated Silver Street. It read "D. MOSES AND SONS – CHEAP CASH STORE." Most buildings were a dark or dull color, with gray and brown being predominant. Some buildings and parts of other buildings were freshly white-washed.

The most brightly-colored building was the Silver Street Hotel and Kitchen. It was directly across from the steamboat landing. The street was widest at this point. No other buildings save one small shed were across from the hotel. The street itself ran for 500 yards or more past the hotel. This area was the general turnaround for wagons and carriages.

The Silver Street Hotel and Kitchen was a bright blue color with white trim. Its porch was wide and spacious and used as a sitting area for most people waiting for the steamboat. It always did brisk business in coffee in the winter and cool drinks in the summer.

Several other narrow, winding dirt streets came off Silver Street, but they were not any length to have names that the Dundee ladies knew. Most went almost to the river.

At the end of Silver Street was the Silver Street Saloon. The rough crowd from the steamboats and under-the-hill workers used this as their watering hole. Riverboat gamblers knew there was always a card game or two with ample pots for interest going on in the saloon.

The Dundee wagon was just approaching the hotel when Gabriel asked, "Missus Dundee, yew ladies gonna waits at the hotel?"

"Yes, Gabriel. Let us down theah, and yew put the wagon over by the landing so yew won't have to carry the trunks so far."

"Mama, why don't we walk down to the saloon and kind of, well, look in as we go by?"

"Mercy, Stelcie. No self-respecting woman would go thcre. Yew hush up about that and git down from this wagon. I don't know where yew git such notions. This younger generation. I don't know what's to happen to yew."

"Aw, Mama. I didn't say go in. All I said was to look inside," said Stelcie as Gabriel helped her down from the wagon seat.

"We'll be having a cool drink of herbal tea while we wait, Gabriel," said Mrs. Dundee. "Is there some water in this wagon for you, Gabriel?"

"Yus, Missus. I be over to de landin'. I be watchin' fer de steamboat."

Gabriel drove the wagon over to the other side of the wide space of street, stopped the team, and turned to look up the Mississippi River for smoke from steamboat stacks.

Mrs. Dundee and Stelcie finished their tea about twenty minutes before the street started stirring with people, and they heard several people shouting, "The steamboat's here! The boat's here!"

Both ladies stood with excitement and moved to the front steps of the hotel along with several other persons awaiting the arrival of the steamboat from Memphis. They watched as the steamboat churned down the river toward the Natchez landing. They stepped onto the muddy street as the boat's whistle blew for the third time. Parts of the street were dry from the hot sun, but yesterday's rain had made some spots wet and muddy for a time. Wagon ruts often held water for days.

The ladies picked their way quite easily, however, across the wide street to the wagon and Gabriel.

"Isn't it grand?" uttered Mrs. Dundee. "I'll never git over the excitement of a riverboat arrivin' at a landin'. Jist look at all the people pourin' out of the stores and businesses to take a gander."

The river boat itself was a twin-stacked stern wheeler painted red, white, and black. It was one of the newer, larger steamboats now on the Mississippi River.

"Dat de biggest boat I ever seed on dis river," said Gabriel in awe as the bow gangplank dropped to the landing.

"My, my! Isn't it pretty?" half-whispered Mrs. Dundee. And then in a louder, normal voice she said, "Look for Sawyer and Solomon."

"Yus'm," answered Gabriel.

The boat crew was scurrying all over the vessel, and passengers were starting to disembark. The Dundees heard one of the riverboat crew say that there would be a two-hour layover. Most passengers would get off the boat for a look at Natchez here below the bluff, and some would walk up the hill to see the scenery and Natchez above the bluff.

"Look at those fancy clothes, Mama. Look at that lady's dress! Oh, Mama, I want one jist like it. Can we ask her where she bought it? Look at that gentleman, Mama. He's so handsome in those clothes!" chattered Stelcie.

The handsome young gentleman turned and looked toward the Dundees. He started walking, picking up his pace.

"It's Sawyer!" squealed Stelcie.

"Mother! Stelcie!"

A few paces later, the handsome young man had swept his mother and sister into his arms and was tightly embracing them.

"Saw! Saw! I can hardly breathe!" said Mrs. Dundee softly.

He released his embrace and stood there, smiling. "Mother, you haven't changed a bit. Not even a single gray hair!"

"Why, Sawyer Dundee. Did yew think I'd be a feeble old woman?" She smiled a mother's smile at her grown son.

"And little Stelcie. You're not a little freckled-faced brat now."

"Oh, Saw, yew always tease me," said Stelcie with a little put-on pout.

"Where's Solomon?" asked Mrs. Dundee.

"He'll be out in a few minutes. He became engaged in a card game this morning. He said he knew he would win, and he was right as usual. They were dealing the last hand when we were told Natchez was in view. He had to return to our room one last time," explained Sawyer. Sawyer turned to Gabriel, "Gabe, my long-time friend, how are you?" He extended his hand to the slave he had grown up with.

"I be happy, Massa Saw," said Gabriel as he shook young Dundee's hand. The two men embraced one another.

"Have you got yourself hitched to a pretty Negress yet?" asked Sawyer. "I saw some pretty ones in Memphis."

"Naw, Massa, I still bes apart from dem womenfolk like dat," said Gabriel, smiling sheepishly.

"Let me look at yew, Saw," said Mrs. Dundee. "Yore a sight for sore eyes."

Sawyer stepped back. He was almost six feet tall. He removed his gentleman's hat. His elegant gray suit with vest and black boots

26

belied his working-man and country-boy background. His dark brown eyes sparkled with happiness at being home with family in Natchez.

"Sawyer, has Solomon picked up that bad habit of card-playing and gambling that his daddy Cain Witcher had?" asked Mrs. Dundee.

"Solomon's card-playing a bad habit? Oh, no, Mother. He doesn't play cards too often. Only when he goes somewhere and watches for a time. Then he says something like he's feeling lucky and knows he's going to win. He always wins when he sits in on the game. He seems to know when he'll win. It's like he can see the future before he sits down at the table. It's uncanny," replied Sawyer. "But I never knew his daddy gambled excessively, Mother."

"Yore Aunt Sarah confided in me. And yore daddy told me, too. He almost always won. But he spent his winnings recklessly. He jist threw away his money. Poor Sarah," Mrs. Dundee whispered. "Now yew two don't repeat what I said—especially not to Solomon. Do yew heah me, Stelcie?"

"Yes, Mama, I won't talk about it," replied Stelcie.

They stood there, looking at the riverboat and watching for Solomon to emerge from the interior of the vessel. A cloud passed in front of the sun and shaded them so drastically that the three of them looked upward at once to see why. A single gray cloud in a blue sky full of great puffy white clouds was passing momentarily over the riverboat landing.

"My, my," Mrs. Dundee said.

Sawyer was the first to look back at the boat. "There's Solomon," he broke the silence, "with the young woman and her father."

Three people were coming toward the gangplank. One was an older man, well-dressed and sophisticated-looking. The shortest of

27

the three was a young woman of about twenty years of age. She wore a pink traveling dress with a caped top about her shoulders. The third person was Solomon. He was just over six feet tall and had dark blue eyes and black hair. He was dressed in a black suit of silk-like material. He carried a black cane and was just putting on his hat when he looked up from his conversation to see the Dundees.

Solomon tipped his hat to the young lady, quickly shook hands with the man, and separated from them.

He called out, "Aunt Laura! Cousin Stelcie!" The bright sun reappeared, and it became hot once more. Solomon had quickened his pace to reach the Dundees.

"Solomon, how glad we are that yew and Sawyer are home," said Mrs. Dundee as she hugged the young man.

"It's good to be home, Aunt Laura," said Solomon. "And Stelcie! Aren't you the lovely young woman now!"

Stelcie blushed and felt her heart palpitate. She hugged her cousin. "Aw, Solomon."

Solomon directed his attention to his Aunt Laura once again. "Why, Aunt Laura, you look younger than when I was last home. You're pretty as a peach."

Laura Dundee felt herself blushing just slightly less than Stelcie. She smiled at Solomon and then Sawyer. "My, my, it is warm out heah," stated Mrs. Dundee. "We must load yore trunks and go."

"Good idea, Mother. There are our trunks and cases now. See, Gabe, the ones there," said Sawyer.

"Yes, Massa Sawyer."

"Gabriel, you rascal," said Solomon. "You look good. They haven't been working you too hard, have they?"

"No, sur," Gabriel said as he went toward the young men's belongings. He, with the young men's help, quickly loaded the wagon.

"Who was the young woman?" asked Stelcie.

"Aren't you the curious one?" replied Solomon. He paused, looking at Stelcie and then Mrs. Dundee. "That was Eve Whitmore. She and her father are from New Orleans. He's in the shipping business there. He's looking for land in this area. They'll be staying in Natchez for a while. They might even relocate here permanently if he finds what he's looking for. Mr. Whitmore was in Memphis on business. I met them on the boat."

"Oh," said Stelcie.

"They'll like Natchez," added Mrs. Dundee. "Yew young men better get on those horses and make haste to the sawmill to see Jeremiah."

"Yes, Massa Sawyer and Massa Solomon, Massa Dundee want both of yew gentlemens to hurries there. He tole me to say so," put in Gabriel.

"We'll go to the house," said Mrs. Dundee. "Go see yore daddy, Son. Go see yore uncle, Solomon."

"Right fast, Mother. I remember that Daddy expects promptness."

"Let's not keep the old man waiting," said Solomon as he mounted his horse and galloped up the hill on Silver Street. Sawyer followed quickly.

The Dundee ladies got up on the wagon seat and sat. Gabriel climbed up, stood behind them, and encouraged the team up the hill. Up above the buildings along the top of the bluffs was a line of scraggly trees and bushes rimming the edge of the bluffs. Solomon and Sawyer had already disappeared from sight and were now riding

29

more slowly through the streets of Natchez toward the sawmill southeast of town.

At the edge of town Solomon turned to Sawyer and said, "Let's run these horses." He slapped Midnight on the rump and yelled, "Come on, Saw!" Midnight sprang forward.

Sawyer goaded Country Boy into a run.

"Massa Dundee! Massa Dundee! They be two riders acomin' lickety-split down de hill towards us," yelled a slave boy, out of breath because he had been running, up to Jeremiah Dundee, who was standing on a pile of pine logs ready to be sawed.

"That's the boys," he said, smiling. He climbed down, strode out to the middle of the mill yard, and stood there, glaring at the oncoming riders. He put his hands on his hipbones and hardened his already stern look and waited. He pushed back his straw hat from his forehead and stifled a grin, just as he remembered doing when they were younger and had stayed out too late at night, and he had waited up for them.

The horses strained to reach the mill yard first. But now both horses felt their riders slack off. There was a man in the middle of the yard. The riders were pulling back to stop them. The horses stopped quickly, their nostrils flaring. Dust billowed around them, their riders, and the man standing in their way.

From the dust came a booming, grating voice, "Yew boys late again?"

The riders dismounted and walked to face the man with the stern voice. The dust settled, and the man glared at Sawyer and Solomon. Jeremiah's stern face broke out in a wide grin. The three men fell into an embrace. "We've missed yew boys!" said Jeremiah.

"It's good to be back."

"Yes, Uncle Jeremiah, we're glad to be back."

"Come over to the shade, boys," Jeremiah Dundee said as he put a hand on the shoulder of each young man and walked between them. "Let me look yew two over."

They moved over to the shade of an old cottonwood tree. Jeremiah sat on a section of a huge log, removed his old hat, and wiped the sweat from his forehead with a faded sleeve that had soaked up perspiration hundreds of times before.

The young men stood before him for further inspection. Jeremiah eyed them up and down and asked, "Do yew boys still know how to work for a living?" He grinned broadly. "Or are yew too educated to sweat in this heah sawmill again?"

"Daddy, you still need help from younger, stronger backs and smarter minds just like before, don't you?

"Yes, sir, we're here and better than ever," added Solomon.

Jeremiah smiled and said, "Well, I made it while yew boys were up north being schooled. But I might find a couple of jobs around here with an ax."

"We're back to help—for the time being, anyway," said Solomon.

"Yes. We hope to help you make a few more dollars. We have a few ideas," added Sawyer.

"Speakin' of ideas," Jeremiah said, "tell me the thinkin' of them Yankees yew boys been associatin' with."

"With regard to what?" asked Sawyer.

"What are they saying about slavery?"

"The Dred Scott decision is still a sore spot. The abolitionists are fit to be tied even now," Sawyer replied.

"Yes, and, Uncle Jeremiah, I went to a theatrical production of *Uncle Tom's Cabin*. I listened to people talk at intermission and afterward. They are convinced that all of us beat and torture the niggers on a daily basis. They don't understand that the niggers are whipped only when they need it," said Solomon.

"Many of the Northerners are becoming more and more consumed with the terribleness of the institution of slavery and its inherent evilness, according to them," Sawyer added.

"Damn Yankees won't listen to reason," injected Solomon. "It's our right to own property. If slavery had proven profitable in the North, they would be arguing for it as an institution there."

"They don't think much of our idea of states' rights, either," Sawyer put in.

"That's somethin'," mused the older Dundee. "What's going to come out of all this?"

"A war, if they want it. We'll fight," said Solomon sharply.

"We don't want no war. No fighting. That's a waste," Jeremiah said quickly. "Ain't no use fightin' over slavery, if I had my druthers. They kin change the Constitution, if'n they want."

"People don't want a war. Do you think?" asked Sawyer.

"They can't abolish slavery without a Constitutional amendment. They can't take our property. It's not right," Solomon added. "We'll fight."

Jeremiah Dundee stood up. "I'm getting' too old to fuss and fight. Besides, it'll never come to a fight. People got enough sense to talk things out and settle the issues peacefully. Ain't no use fightin' over slavery. Jist hold yore horses. No need to git dandered up yet. They can change the Constitution, if'n they kin git the votes from the states."

32

The older man and the two younger men stood silently, looking at one another.

"You got a lot of work today?" Sawyer finally asked.

"Yes. Yes. But I'll be in early. Yew boys go on to the house, and I'll be there inside an hour. We'll finish this load, and I'll let the foreman take over and finish here. I'm anxious to talk more to yew fellows about what them Yankees are thinkin' 'bout us. Yew can tell me all the news and politics then. Glad yew're back, boys." He shook hands with the young men and said, "Git on home. Beulah's fixin' up a big supper. She will be anxious to see both of yew." He turned and strode to the other side of the mill.

Solomon and Sawyer looked at him as he moved away. "Solomon, do you think that people will fight, that there'll be a war?"

"There will be a war, a long and bloody struggle," Solomon replied slowly in a most serious manner. "I know it." He now whispered so low that Sawyer did not hear him say, "I know it. I saw war in a dream."

Sawyer looked at him quizzically.

"I just know it," Solomon said loudly.

Each young man looked at the other for a few moments. Sawyer broke the silence when he said, "Let's go home."

They mounted their horses and headed for home, riding briskly. "Look there, through the trees. See the house," said Solomon.

"A welcome sight indeed," Sawyer added. The horses picked up their pace. The young men turned the horses onto the house road and rode up to a sycamine tree. Solomon stopped Midnight first, and Sawyer halted Country Boy. Solomon pointed to the sycamine tree, saying, "Remember what Grandma Dundee said about that sycamine when it was just a scraggly thing?"

33

"Yeah. She used it as an example of faith. It and the mustard seed. She wanted us to have a strong faith in God. She wanted it to grow like the tiny mustard seed."

They both looked at the sycamine tree and thought about Grandma Dundee in her rocking chair on the porch and her Bible reading to them as little ones.

"She always said it would be easy for you to figure out, to understand what she meant, Solomon. Was it?"

"I don't rightly know if I ever did, or ever will," replied Solomon, who seemed deep in thought while staring intently at the sycamine. He remembered everything Grandma Dundee had ever shared with him, especially those things she spoke about only to him—the dreams of the future, his birthing caul, superstitions that could be true about him—all of it.

Sawyer glanced upward toward the house and back down at the sycamine just in time to see its leaves shake. He felt no breeze at the moment, no stirring of the wind. "I've been out in the hot sun too long. I thought the sycamine's leaves were shaking. The heat's making me imagine things. Let's get inside for a cool drink," he said as he made Country Boy lift up his head from nibbling a clump of grass.

"Leaves shaking? It is hot," said Solomon. "I'm right behind you, cousin." But Solomon lagged behind for a few seconds more and eyed the sycamine as old Grandma Dundee had told him to. He saw the leaves shake again. He felt no breeze this time either. But he did feel something, a strange sort of energy or vitality or something within him. Grandma Dundee's words rang in his ears, "It'll be easy for yew, little Witcher. Use what yew got, boy." He followed Sawyer now.

They went behind the house where they were met by Gabriel, who took their horses after they had dismounted. Gabriel shouted toward the kitchen's back door, "Beulah woman! Beulah woman! The young massas be here!"

Solomon and Sawyer looked at the kitchen door. Beulah burst from the doorway, saying, "Massa Sawyer! Massa Solomon! Bless yore hearts! We's so happy yew to home agin." She rushed over to Sawyer first, hesitating momentarily as she tried to decide whether to hug the young man or not. She looked anxiously into his eyes. "Massa Sawyer."

Sawyer reached out to her. That was the signal she needed. She embraced the young man of the present and the boy of the past.

"Beulah, I'm glad to be back. To see you. To be home again. To stay," Sawyer said to her. "I missed your cooking." Beulah beamed her toothy grin.

Beulah turned to Solomon when he spoke. "It is good to be back." He put his hand on her shoulder and then his arm around her shoulder and back. There was an affection in the half-embrace, but Beulah sensed a certain aloofness of restraint. There was something else in his demeanor, his persona, that was different from the last time he had hugged her. She could feel it in her bones and thought of things she had overhead Grandma Dundee say to Solomon. Sensing her heart beating more rapidly in her chest, she smiled up at him anyway.

"Yew, young mens, come on into de house. Gabriel done put yore traveling cases and trunks in yore rooms. The Missus and Miss Stelcie be waiting in the parlor for yew. Comes on in. I be cooking a big supper for everyones tonight." She shepherded the young men into the house and through the kitchen.

They walked into the parlor.

"There's warshing water in yore room. Go up, see if yore rooms are in order. Yew can warsh off some of the dust from the road and then come back down. Jeremiah's coming in early today, he said," Laura Dundee clucked like a mother hen.

The young men dutifully went upstairs. By the time they came down, Jeremiah was in from the sawmill, ready to talk once more.

That night they ate the hearty meal that Beulah had prepared for the homecoming. They talked of family matters at the table, and then they moved to the parlor to talk politics.

Stelcie sat by her mother, who did little talking now. Laura Dundee listened, and Stelcie followed suit.

"But the states have the right to help owners maintain their slave property. It's our constitutional right to own property. Slaves are property," said Solomon adamantly. "The Yankees are just jealous of the way we live. Their factory system makes slaves out of its workers. The conditions those people work under are terrible. When a worker gets sick or hurt, the owners don't take care of them the way we do our slaves. They just get others to take their places and forget about the sick or hurt."

Stelcie, who had been soaking up all the talk about the Northerners and their attitudes toward the South, burst out, "Damn Yankees!"

"Stelcie! Yew mind yore tongue, young lady!" responded Laura Dundee. "Refined ladies do not say such words."

"I'm sorry." Then she said under her breath, "Damn Northerners."

"Stelcie, mind your manners," added Jeremiah with a very stern look on his face.

"It's time for us to retire for the night, anyway, Stelcie," said Mrs. Dundee.

"Mother, please, let's stay up for a while longer."

"No, dear, let's allow the menfolk time to themselves. We'll talk more tomorrow. Good night, all," said Laura as she kissed Jeremiah. Stelcie kissed her father and followed Mrs. Dundee out of the parlor. Mrs. Dundee's voice came through the doorway, "Now, Jeremiah, don't stay up too late. The boys are tired from their journey, and yew'll be up before daylight to go to the sawmill. Yew need yore rest."

"Yes, Laura. Good night, dear," he said softly with a smile.

Sawyer smiled, too.

Solomon said in a low voice, "Women."

Jeremiah looked at the young man and spoke, "What's the reaction where y'all were about Kansas?"

Sawyer was first to speak, "That, too, riled up many people. But most deplored the killing and violence."

"Yes, but they still blamed the South for all of it," put in Solomon.

"Not everyone," Sawyer rebutted.

"Most of the Yankees thought it, even if they didn't say it. You remember the looks we got when some people found out we were from Natchez, Mississippi," said Solomon. "It was uncomfortable, to say the least."

"Yes, and the one time you lost your head and almost had a dozen or so ruffians—"

"I don't want to talk about it. It still makes me mad," broke in Solomon.

"Well, well, boys," said Mr. Dundee, "I'll bet y'all two had some awkward moments."

"It wasn't really a problem except for a couple of incidents. I suppose we could have avoided some places and not had the—"

"No one's gonna tell me where I can't go and what I can't say," interrupted Solomon, louder now. His face was reddening.

"Hold on! Calm down, young man," Mr. Dundee said. "Yew'll disturb the whole house. Besides, yew are home now. Yew are back in Natchez."

Solomon went silent, and the natural color gradually came back into his face. In a few minutes more, he rejoined the conversation. The men talked well past midnight.

Finally, stifling a yawn, Sawyer asked, "Daddy, you want us to work in the morning?"

"As a matter of fact, I do," Mr. Dundee said, "but I promised Stelcie I'd let her take y'all over to Clifton to meet her friend Miriam. She rather wants to show off her handsome brother and handsome cousin. Y'all have to accompany her, or I'll never hear the end of it. Yew men can start at the sawmill Monday morning. How about it?"

"Fine."

"Yes, Uncle Jeremiah."

They walked out of the parlor, up the stairs, exchanged "good-nights" at the head of the stairs, and went to their respective rooms.

It was mid-morning when Sawyer came downstairs looking for breakfast. He went into the kitchen where Beulah was bustling about, readying things for the noon meal. He slipped up behind her just before she turned around. "Morning, Beulah," he said crisply as she turned.

She shrieked and dropped a black kettle. Then she cackled out loud and scolded, "Massa Sawyer, I done thinked yew and Massa

Solomon be outgrowed scarin' me like yew done whens yews two be boys." Beulah grinned from ear to ear.

"Somebody say my name?" asked Solomon as he came into the kitchen.

"I be saying it. Yew two mens still boys inside when Beulah in dis kitchen. Massa Sawyer done scare de daylights outta me dis mornin' de way when yew be little."

"You still have some breakfast in this kitchen, Beulah?" asked Sawyer.

"Biscuits and bacon and grits I always got," replied Beulah as she floated here and there in the kitchen, producing a plate of biscuits, a rack of bacon, and a pot of grits. "Sits here. I be warmin' de food in a hurry for my young Massas."

The young men sat while Beulah scurried about with the food. In a few minutes the men were eating and bantering with Beulah.

That afternoon they were riding with Stelcie into Natchez on their way to Clifton. Stelcie constantly chattered, telling them of the people who lived in the houses along the way.

Stelcie, riding sidesaddle, wore a calico dress with a light brown broad-brimmed hat. At one point she said, "Let's go by Magnolia Hall. It's been recently completed. It's jist plain beautiful!"

They turned their horses and in a few minutes' time rode in front of the structure. "Isn't it jist grand?" exclaimed Stelcie.

Magnolia Hall was beautiful. Even the young men felt its grandeur as they passed it.

"I'm going to have something like that one day," said Solomon.

"I'll visit you all the time, cousin Solomon," Stelcie said.

"You do that," Solomon replied.

39

"There's talk about a great house that Dr. Haller Nutt wants to build. He's seeking a Northern architect to draw up the plans," said Stelcie. "And he hopes the building will start next year some time."

"He's accumulated more money while we were away, I'll bet," Solomon mused.

"Daddy said that Dr. Nutt bought more land and is planting more cotton than ever. And I overheard that his investments in the North make him more and more money," Stelcie added.

"Maybe he'll buy some lumber from us to build this big mansion," Sawyer said.

"Daddy'll be happy."

They rode on. "It's not far to Clifton. Miriam is such a nice person. She and I are good, good friends. I can't wait until she meets y'all. And the party tomorrow evening. It'll be grand. I can't wait. Daddy bought me a new dress. I hope I'll be as pretty as Miriam. Will yew two dance with me if nobody else asks me?"

Sawyer and Solomon assured Stelcie of her loveliness and that she would have more than enough dance partners.

"Did Aunt Laura say that Miriam was the Surgets' niece?" Solomon asked.

"Yes. The Surgets have no children of their own. Miriam is Mr. Surget's niece from Memphis. She's visiting for a few months. She's a fine young lady. Y'all will like her."

They rounded a curve in the road, and in the distance was Clifton.

"Oh, Clifton is so beautiful! Jist look at it!" exclaimed Stelcie in her usual dreamy voice.

Clifton was indeed beautiful. Its setting was near the high, steep bluffs of the Mississippi River. The mansion arrested attention.

40

It dominated its surroundings except for the Mississippi River itself. The river and Clifton complemented one another. It was as though both could feel the spirit of the other, and a sort of bond existed between the two.

"It's been a long time since we were here. Clifton is still breathtaking," said Sawyer.

"It certainly is," Solomon agreed. "The orchard and the other buildings are something in themselves. The summer house and greenhouse look larger."

Has Mr. Surget added any art pieces to his collection?" asked Sawyer.

"Yes. He's traveled in Europe since y'all have been away in school. This is the first summer he and Mrs. Surget have remained home. Miriam is why. They're happy to have her with them," replied Stelcie.

They now rode on the broad carriageway that led to and past the high-columned portico. Their horses' hooves crackled on the gravel and sea shells that made up the carriageway.

"Smell those magnolias. And that crepe myrtle," said Stelcie, breathing deeply. "Yew should be out on the terrace on a spring afternoon. The scent and sights are beguiling. It's jist dreamy. So peaceful and calm."

"I had forgotten how elegant Clifton is," said Solomon. "Just look out there. The river. The gardens. The terraces. And the house. It's unbelievable."

"Like a fairyland," added Stelcie.

Just then a slave came up to them to take their horses. "Afternoon, Miss Stelcie. Afternoon, gentlemen," said another slave who came out of the front doorway onto the portico. He was dressed elegantly as a house servant and was obviously much more refined than the average domestic slave. "Come in. Please come in. I'll send word to Miss Miriam and the Master that yew are here," he said as he showed them through a wide hall and into the parlor. He stepped back into the doorway and called in a firm voice, "Nazlee! Nazlee! Fetch yoreself to Miss Miriam and Master Surget to say that company is here. It's Miss Stelcie and two young gentlemen."

They heard footsteps scurrying.

"Please sit. Miss Miriam will be here shortly," he said as he exited the room.

While waiting, they looked about the parlor. The room was large with a high ceiling and had two windows reaching down to the floor. They were opened, and one could walk out onto the green grassy terrace. The walls were hung with paintings, and busts rested upon fine cherry wood stands and oak tables. There were two large plush sofas and five exquisitely detailed chairs. A tall bookcase stood between the open windows, and a full-length wood-framed mirror decorated the wall behind where Stelcie sat. The breeze from the open windows gently puffed the sheer lace panel curtains away from the drapes and caused the glass chandelier to tinkle softly.

"Stelcie, Stelcie. Hello," said Miriam as she entered the parlor. Miriam was a raven-haired young woman with hazel eyes. She was five feet tall with a slender build. She wore a pale blue dress that was slightly off her shoulders and carried a small silk fan.

Solomon and Sawyer rose at the greeting of Stelcie and smiled. Miriam returned their smiles and continued, "You handsome gentlemen must be Sawyer and Solomon. I'm delighted to meet y'all. I'm Miriam Surget."

"I'm Saw—"

"My name is Solomon Witcher, and I'm at your service, Miriam. You are even lovelier than my dear cousin Stelcie described you," Solomon said as he took her extended hand and raised it to his lips to kiss.

"My, my," said Miriam as she felt her face blush. "I wasn't expecting such a refined gentleman." She put her hand back down at her side and felt her heart palpitate as she looked directly in Solomon's eyes. "My, my," she repeated as she put one hand on her bosom and fanned her face with the other.

"And this is my brother Sawyer," said Stelcie, directing Miriam's attention to her brother.

Miriam extended her hand and then turned her face to Sawyer. Sawyer grasped her hand and shook it as delicately as he could. "You are lovely," he said.

"Why, thank you, Sawyer," she replied as Mr. Surget walked into the room.

"Good afternoon, all. Stelcie, yew about ready for the party tomorrow evening?"

Everyone turned toward Mr. Surget.

Introductions were exchanged, and talk of the party was the order of the day with arrangements finalized for the double birthday party for the young women. It was to begin at five o'clock and be on the south lawn near the garden avenue.

Afterward, when Solomon, Sawyer, and Stelcie were on the portico, waiting for their horses to be brought around, Miriam said, "I hope it doesn't rain tomorrow. That would spoil our party."

"We never know about the weather here," said Stelcie.

"It won't rain. Look at the sky. It won't rain," said Solomon with a certain guarantee in his voice.

"I don't know about that," Sawyer said.

Farewells were said, and the three visitors began their way home.

In Natchez Solomon unexpectedly said to Sawyer and Stelcie, "Y'all go on home. I'm going by the hotel where Miss Whitmore and her father said they would stay. He said that he would rent a house as soon as he could. That man struck me as someone who doesn't waste time."

"Miss Whitmore, huh?" said Stelcie. She pondered for a moment. "Solomon, why don't yew invite her and her daddy to our party? The Surgets said Miriam and I could invite anyone we wished. We can welcome them to Natchez. I'll tell Mama and Daddy to add them to our guest list."

"That's a good idea," Sawyer said. "Why don't you invite both to the party?"

Solomon grinned. "I'll do just that." He galloped away, and Sawyer and Stelcie continued home.

Sawyer spoke first. "Well, little sister, did Solomon and I measure up? What did Miriam think?"

"She likes both of yew. She thinks yew are quite nice, and Solomon, she—"

"He really impressed her, didn't he? He had her blushing and gushing from the start. He just overflowed with charm. I saw it. Didn't you?"

"Oh, Saw. Yew know that I—"

"That's the way he always is, especially with females. It's his nature. It's just something that he was born with. I've seen the same thing happen over and over while we were up north in school. I wish I had some of his natural charm or whatever you want to call it."

44

Sawyer paused. The horses made the only noises as they ambled down the road.

"But, Saw, yew're a kind, considerate person," Stelcie said.

"Yeah."

"Yew are."

"I still wish I knew Solomon's secret. Why, he can even treat the ladies unkindly, and they'll forgive him in the time it takes a cat to purr."

"What? What do yew mean?"

"Solomon's had several girlfriends while we were away. I thought that he was about to be married a couple of times, but things didn't go that way in the end. He had quarrels with some females about his being overly friendly with others. But, in the end, he could talk his way out of any situation with the ladies."

"Why did—"

"I'm talking too much about things my little sister doesn't need to worry her pretty little head about. But I still wish the ladies would gush over me the way they do over Solomon. I'll have to learn his secret one day."

"Saw, yew're my handsome brother. Yew don't have to worry," Stelcie said sweetly. "Now tell me, brother dear, have yew gotten me a birthday present yet?"

Sawyer grinned. "Well, I have a present. It was going to be yours, but I simply must give Miriam something after meeting her. Don't you agree? It would be unmannerly of me to attend her party at her house and not give her a present, wouldn't it?"

"Saw!"

"I could always get you a honeybee in a flower."

"Goobers and grits, Sawyer Dundee, yew stop teasing," said Stelcie with the smile of a little sister who has said the same words hundreds of times in the past.

They rode on and were almost home when Sawyer asked, "How has Daddy's health been? I thought I detected some concern in Mama's voice last night as y'all were retiring?"

"He's been fine. He works all the time. Too much according to Mama. But he's not complained of feeling poorly. I think Mama jist remembers Grandfather's untimely passing that hot summer day at the sawmill up near Corinth. She always says that Daddy's just like Grandpa."

"We're back now. We can help take some of the work off Daddy's shoulders. Things'll be better."

"Yes."

"The party tomorrow is just what we all need. We'll have a fine time," said Sawyer.

They turned their horses onto the road to their house.

Sawyer pointed and said, "Look, there's Mama sitting on the porch. We'll tell her what Miriam said about the last-minute party preparations. Mama will enjoy the party, too."

Laura Dundee saw her children and waved.

Across town Solomon rode down Silver Street and dismounted in front of the Silver Street Hotel and Kitchen. He tied Midnight's reins to a post and entered the hotel.

He was just about to walk to the registration desk when he heard his name called. He turned and saw the Whitmores coming down the stairway.

"I was about to inquire of you," Solomon said, walking over to meet them. He shook hands with Mr. Whitmore and smiled at Eve.

Mr. Whitmore stated, "We were going to dine here at the hotel's kitchen. Won't yew join us?"

"Yes, Solomon, please do," echoed Eve.

"I'm delighted to do so. They've always prepared excellent food here," Solomon replied. "This way, Mr. Whitmore." Solomon gestured to Mr. Whitmore and then extended his arm to Eve to escort her into the dining area.

The dining room, filled with tables of various sizes and shapes, was rather spacious. Tables could seat five or six individuals. The room could accommodate about sixty patrons. Cream-colored linen tablecloths matched the curtains, and a vase of freshly cut wildflowers sat in the middle of each table.

A black server seated the Whitmores and Solomon at a corner table and left them each a menu. He returned shortly for their order. While waiting for their food to be prepared and served, Solomon turned the conversation to the next day's activities. "What do you have planned for tomorrow, Mr. Whitmore?"

"I must complete the arrangements for us to procure a residence on the hill. It's a nice little summer house for us to live in while I examine the business opportunities here in Natchez. I should be finished by noon. Eve was to accompany me. Why do yew inquire?"

"Because," said Solomon, "you are invited to a double birthday party at Clifton. For my cousin Stelcie and her friend Miriam, the niece of the Surgets. Will you accept and attend?"

"What a delight!" Eve said. "May we attend, father?"

"Why, yes. I've heard that Clifton is one of the most elegant and stately homes in Natchez and the entire South. And that the Surgets are such gracious hosts," Mr. Whitmore said. "And perhaps he can provide some insight concerning investments."

"And you will meet many of Natchez's fine families and some fine people from the Louisiana side of the river. Some more business connections, I might add," stated Solomon.

"Yew are right, my boy," smiled Mr. Whitmore.

"But, Daddy, I don't have a dress for the occasion. And what about gifts for the two birthday girls?"

"Yew can shop in the morning while I conclude my business," said Mr. Whitmore matter-of-factly.

"Good, Daddy. It'll work out in a splendid fashion. I saw some shops earlier today."

Waiters brought their meal, and they began eating and made idle conversation. At the end of the meal, Mr. Whitmore looked at Solomon. "Eve will need an escort other than her old daddy, don't you think, Solomon?" At this suggestion, Eve smiled and looked at Solomon.

"But, of course, she does. May I request the honor of your company, my dear Eve, at the Surgets' home tomorrow evening?" Solomon said with sparkling eyes.

"You're too kind, gracious sir. I am pleased to go with you."

"I'll arrange for a carriage for us here at the hotel. We won't be in the house until Monday. What time should we be ready to go?" Mr. Whitmore said.

Solomon answered his question and then walked the Whitmores back to the stairs to the second floor. He bid them good night, walked out of the hotel, and turned toward the Silver Street Saloon after getting Midnight's reins and tugging for the horse to follow.

Loud piano music emanated from the saloon. Midnight snorted and then whinnied. "Music too loud, boy?" said Solomon. "I guess I'll hitch your rein right here for a time." He wrapped Midnight's bridle rein around one of the rails and patted his horse's withers as he left him.

The music was loud but inviting to Solomon. He liked being around people having a good time. The saloon wasn't even half full because of the early hour. A large well-stocked bar stretched the entire length of the room. Near one end behind the bar was a closed door. Red drapes framed the large front windows that he had looked in before entering. All the tables were round with four or five chairs at them. At the far end of the big room was a small elevated stage. Its deep red curtains were drawn loosely. A light red wallpaper was on the walls above the dark brown wainscoting. Two chandeliers, assisted by flickering lamps along each wall, lit the room.

Solomon gave the entire room a quick perusal. Three tables had solitary men seated at them, slowly sipping drinks. Several other tables had three or four people sitting and drinking and talking. One table near the stage had three nicely dressed gentlemen playing a game of cards. A few people, including a saloon girl, were leaning on the bar near the entrance. Solomon walked up to the bar and asked for whiskey. Momentarily the bartender complied with his request, and as Solomon put his money on the bar, he asked, "Is that card game open to anybody who wants to play?"

"I dunno. I suppose so," answered the big, burly barkeep. "Yew'll have to ask them gents."

Solomon took his drink and headed to the far table, saying, "I feel like I am going to win me a few hands."

A new hand had been dealt, so Solomon stood watching the three men handle their cards. The game was a friendly low-stakes affair. He watched two more hands before asking to sit in. The three agreed that another player would make for a more interesting game. Solomon sat, took out his money, and dealt the cards. The first hand he had no good combination of cards. The second hand he knew he had the winning cards but folded so the gentlemen directly across from him would win. When the man showed his cards, Solomon saw that he himself actually had the winning cards which he had just put face down on the table. He knew he would win now.

Solomon played the friendly game for an hour, winning almost a hundred dollars. He grew bored with the game and deliberately folded away two winning hands. He looked up from the new dealer and saw a pretty blonde young woman who obviously worked there, standing behind the man across from him. She smiled at Solomon, and he winked at her. As Solomon won the next five hands, the blonde woman moved around the table closer to him.

"Why don't you let me buy you a drink over at the bar?" Solomon said to her as he raked in the pot from his last winning hand. He folded his paper money, pocketed the coins, and said, "Thanks, gents. Another game, another time?" He followed the young woman as she sashayed to the bar. "What's your name?"

"My name is Cammie. What's yours?"

"Solomon."

"The wise king from the Bible?" Cammie toyed with him. "What is a holy man doing in this saloon?"

Cammie looked at Solomon, directly in his eyes. Her teasing smile faded from her face as his eyes brightened, and he said, "A wise man, I hope. A king, I wish. A holy man, you hope not." His eyes brightened even more. He took a half step toward her.

She grinned weakly. Her heart pounded in her breast. He smiled a beguiling smile. He looked down at her suddenly heaving bosom.

"What'll it be?" inquired the bartender, breaking the intensity of the moment.

Solomon turned to him and answered, "A whiskey and a bottle of your best wine for Cammie."

"That'll cost yew."

"Fetch it for her. Bring it now. Here's money," snapped Solomon, obviously annoyed.

Cammie was breathing normally now and moved closer to Solomon. She put her arm around his waist. "I've never met anyone quite like yew, Solomon," she said slowly and softly.

But Solomon, who had seen the door behind the bar open and close, was preoccupied with what he had seen. There was a poker game in the back room.

"Solomon," said Cammie again. She grasped his arm. "Solomon."

"I'm still feeling lucky. I know I can win," he said to her.

"What?"

He looked at her. "What's going on in that room back there?" He turned completely to her and gathered her hands into his. "What's back there?"

"In the room? It's a private room. A private game. Invitation only. They bet big money," she explained.

"Who invites?"

"Only the owner and a few other people around here. Some of the riverboat captains can get people in for a serious game. They say that it's cash money only," she stated.

"You don't go in there? You can't get me in?"

"Me? Get yew in that game? Oh, no. I cain't. I've only been in there three times myself. And only then because a certain gentleman requested that I be allowed to go in," Cammie hastily said.

"Where's the owner? I'll ask him. I'll demand to get in that game!" stated Solomon. "I have money."

"Oh, no, that won't work. Other people have tried it. There's no way. Yew have to be invited. Yew must have lots of money. When I watched the game, several thousand dollars changed hands each time."

Solomon calmed himself and asked, "What was the ante?"

"Fifty dollars."

"Fifty dollars?"

"Yes."

"How often do they play?"

"At least once a month. Sometimes more. It depends on the riverboat passengers. The same people usually play. The owner of the saloon plays every time."

"I suppose I'll need more cash than I now have. And I'll have to get to know some of the regular players. I'll play with them one day," stated Solomon. He poured Cammie a little more wine and then put the bottle to his mouth and drank down the remainder. He turned his back to the bar and leaned on it. Cammie did likewise.

Solomon surveyed the room and its patrons. He was silent and sullen.

After a few minutes Cammie said, "Get us another bottle of wine and let's slip out to walk on the riverbank. The moon shimmering on the river is beautiful." She put her hand on his, squeezed it, and said, "Solomon."

He turned, looked at her, smiled and motioned for the bartender. "Won't you be missed?"

"No. Robert will cover for me. He owes me," she said as the bartender came over. "Robert, I'll be back." She winked and flashed him a big smile.

"Another bottle of wine," said Solomon.

"Meet me outside at the corner. I'll be right there. I just can't be seen leaving with yew. I'll bring the wine. Hurry."

Solomon walked slowly across to the door and exited to the boardwalk in the front. He stood, looking at the riverboat landing and listening to the music, talk, and laughter from inside. He turned to walk to the corner. Cammie appeared.

"Come on," she whispered, motioning to him.

Solomon leisurely strolled over to Cammie, and she grabbed his hand and tugged him off the boardwalk away from the lights of the saloon into the soft light of the moon. Solomon could see a worn path leading into the trees along the bank of the Mississippi. Moonlight shimmered in the current of the river. The high bluffs seemed to reach to the stars. Cammie kept pulling Solomon along. He looked at her as they moved along the path. She was pretty. Her dress she had hiked up somewhat in front with her other hand, so she could watch her footing. Her shawl had fallen down around her upper arms, revealing her bare shoulders. They looked so creamy white in the moonlight.

Solomon glanced back at the saloon. Its light seemed so harsh as they disappeared into the trees.

"Where are we going?" asked Solomon.

"A little farther. Just a little farther. There's a beautiful place jist up ahead. We'll have to go upward a bit," Cammie said over her shoulder.

Solomon felt the incline. Cammie was breathing heavily by the time she stopped and turned around and said, "Look." She pointed out over the river.

It was breathtaking. The moon, the stars, the river. The man and the woman were silent, but the night was not. They could hear the insects, the frogs, and the other creatures of the night. The sounds engulfed them. Cammie whispered, "The night is beautiful."

They stood motionless until Cammie said, "Let's sit and talk." She sat on a patch of grass and pulled Solomon down beside her. "Solomon, do yew like me?"

"Do I like you?"

"Do yew? I mean, do yew really like me? I'm just a saloon girl. I'm . . . "

Yes, I like you, Cammie. I'm here with you," said Solomon.

"Yew're jist saying that." She took the wine bottle from Solomon and opened it. She drank several swallows and thrust it into Solomon's hands.

"Cammie."

She looked into his eyes, and he looked back, studying her eyes with an intensity that made her heart race.

"You love someone. You love someone else. Someone who didn't return your love. I can sense it," said Solomon softly.

"How do yew know that? How do yew know?"

"I just know," Solomon said. "What happened?"

Cammie said nothing, but tears sprang to her eyes and rolled down her cheeks. She leaned into Solomon's arms, and he cradled her and rocked her gently.

Her tears ended, and she raised up to look at Solomon's face in the moonlight. He smiled at her, and she smiled back, weakly at first. She felt warm inside and basked in Solomon's favor. He leaned to kiss her, and she felt a tide of passion well within her. She forgot about the past. She forgot about everything and everybody but Solomon. She stood, the waxing moon behind her. Solomon watched as her shawl dropped to the ground. She unfastened the buttons at the back of her dress and let it slide down around her ankles. Solomon rose to his feet as well, Cammie stepped out of her dress and into his arms.

Solomon came downstairs a little before noon, just in time to eat an abbreviated mid-day meal with the others.

As they sat, Stelcie asked, "How's that Miss Whitmore? Did yew git to see her last evening? Yew must have. Yew certainly stayed out late last night, didn't yew?"

Solomon looked at her with a smile. "Female cousins surely ask a lot of questions."

Laura Dundee chided Stelcie. "Stelcie, yew pull yore nose out of Solomon's personal business. Solomon's his own man."

"Thank you, Aunt Laura."

"Well, at least yew can tell me if yew asked her to our party, cain't yew?" returned Stelcie.

"Oh, I imagine she'll be there," inserted Sawyer. "I don't know of any female turning down one of Solomon's invites to go to a party."

"Sawyer's right," said Solomon. "Miss Whitmore will be there. And so will her father."

"Fine," said Laura Dundee. "It will be a nice way to welcome them to Natchez. I am anxious to git to know them."

55

"Did yew tell them the time it begins? Do they know how to git to Clifton?" asked Stelcie.

"Questions, questions, my little cousin. Calm yourself. I shall accompany them to Clifton and shall be Eve's escort for the evening," related Solomon.

Sawyer said with a sigh, "That's the usual happening. Cousin Solomon has a pretty girl to go to the party with, and I'll be standing and looking while the music is playing." He grinned. "You think there will be some unattached young ladies there?"

They all laughed good-naturedly. The conversation turned to preparations for the party. Beulah hustled the family about in order to get things done.

After the ladies had left to make their preparations at Clifton, Sawyer and Solomon sat on the front porch, waiting for Jeremiah to return home to get ready for the party themselves. As they sat, Sawyer looked up at the few white clouds in the blue sky and said, "It looks like it won't rain. The party will go well."

"I told you it wouldn't rain," Solomon said.

They watched the clouds float across the sky. Solomon cleared his throat and said, "Saw, how long do you think it'll be before Uncle Jeremiah goes through with his promise to make us partners in his sawmill business?"

"Oh, I don't really know. He's always told us that. I think we'll work a while; and when we learn the business through and through, he'll want to step back from the workload some and give us more free rein. It'll be a year, maybe two."

"Uncle Jeremiah won't step back from work. He's always worked. Every day I can remember. It's in his being. He has to work, or he'll die."

"Oh, he'll have plenty to do. He's got his cotton land to work. He acquired more acreage while we were away. And remember what we've discussed before. Maybe we can sell him on the idea of a foundry. I bet there would be need for an additional one in this area. Opportunities are here. This city's growing. Haven't you noticed how many more houses and businesses are here now than when we went up north? And steamboats are plying the Mississippi River in greater numbers."

"You're right. You've got the business head between the two of us. You make sense," Solomon said.

"Daddy'll be fair by us. I know it. You know it. It'll just take some time. Have faith, Solomon," Sawyer stated.

Solomon was quiet. He gazed out at the sycamine tree. He could hear in the back of his mind old Grandma Dundee and her words about faith.

The sounds of a galloping horse interrupted his thoughts. Jeremiah Dundee turned up the road to his house. He shouted, "Hello, men. Are yew ready to get into them fancy clothes and go flirt with the pretty ladies?"

Solomon and Sawyer stood. "Sounds good to me," said Sawyer, smiling.

The three men talked for a short time about what was going on at the mill. Solomon and Sawyer walked around the house to the stable with Jeremiah to rest his horse for a time and to saddle Midnight and Country Boy. Then they walked up to the house to ready themselves for the party. Solomon was first to get changed and ready. He told the other men that he must go ahead to the hotel on Silver Street to meet the Whitmores. His horse had been brought up to the house, and he soon had Midnight trotting away. A short time later Sawyer and Jeremiah were on their horses on their way to Clifton.

It was half past three when they dismounted their horses at Clifton. Two servants took their horses, and another directed them to where the Surgets and Dundees were.

"Ah, Jeremiah, how are yew this pleasant day?" said Frank Surget, extending his hand and clasping Jeremiah's in a warm, friendly handshake. "And Sawyer, how are yew, young man?"

Sawyer shook hands with Mr. Surget.

From the other end of the terrace came Laura Dundee and Charlotte Surget. They exchanged greetings. Charlotte was in her late thirties, about fifteen years younger than her husband. She wasn't beautiful, but she was far from plain with a certain nobleness about her. She was tall for a woman, with refined features. Her eyes were a captivating blue in color. She possessed a gentle, somewhat musical voice, and a genuine sweet smile that she shared with everyone, old and young, rich and poor, man and woman, white and black.

Stelcie and Miriam came up. The four women were all dressed in hoop-skirted dresses made of light fabric. The younger ladies' dresses were made to bare their shoulders with low necklines in front. Laura Dundee's dress was full-bodice with a much less daring neckline than the girls'. Mrs. Surget's dress resembled that of the younger ones. Each woman wore a broad-brimmed hat that matched their dress—the Dundees in similar shades of red, Miriam in a brilliant yellow, and Mrs. Surget in lavender.

"My, my, aren't you ladies lovely? You make my heart race," Sawyer said as he put his hand on his chest.

"Where's Solomon?" asked Miriam, looking disappointed.

"He'll be here in a while," said Stelcie. "He'll be accompanying the Whitmores, some new people in Natchez. Mr. Whitmore's a businessman from New Orleans. I think he's looking for cotton land around here. Solomon met them on the riverboat."

"There are the people you told me about, Laura?" asked Charlotte Surget. "I'm glad we have included them on our guest list. Now tell me about Mrs. Whitmore."

"There's not a Mrs. Whitmore. She died years back. His daughter Eve is with Mr. Whitmore," Stelcie said.

"His daughter," Miriam said, mortified.

"Yes, his daughter. I saw her at the landing the day Saw and Solomon came back. She's lovely, at least from the distance I saw her."

"Oh, my," said Miriam.

"They will arrive later. Let's go up to yore room to freshen up a bit. I'm simply wilting in this heat. Come on, Miriam," said Stelcie. The two younger ladies went toward the house.

"Excuse us, gentlemen. We have things to see to," Charlotte said as she and Laura Dundee turned away and walked over to a nearby table.

"So Mr. Whitmore is looking for investment opportunities?" asked Frank Surget.

"I think he's in the shipping business," Sawyer said.

"We'll introduce him to some friends of ours tonight, eh, Jeremiah?" said Surget.

"He'll meet lots of folks at this celebration," Jeremiah added.

The musicians had arrived, had assembled themselves in their area, and soon were tuning their instruments for playing. At five o'clock the music began, greeting the Surgets' party guests. In the front of the musicians was a large open area of the lawn for dancing. Other guests were coming in. Carriages were waiting in line on the front carriageway to let down their passengers.

59

Laura Dundee and Charlotte Surget had removed their hats and were greeting guests, as were Jeremiah and Frank. Miriam and Stelcie had reappeared and were standing a short distance from their relatives. They, too, were extending greetings to the people coming in until one young man asked Miriam to dance. She accepted, and Stelcie moved beside her parents until Sawyer, who was talking to an old friend, noticed and went over to ask her to dance. She also accepted the invitation.

"I told yew I wouldn't be asked to dance," said Stelcie to her brother.

"The party's just beginning, Stelcie. Don't worry. People are still arriving. Don't fret, little sister. It leaves lines in your forehead."

Her face softened, and she smiled. "Big brothers do come in handy—sometimes."

"I've told you that many times," said Sawyer, "but you wouldn't believe—"

Sawyer felt a hand tapping his shoulder. He turned his head to look, halting their dancing.

"May I cut in, kind sir?" asked a handsome young man.

"Why, uh, yes, of course, you may," Sawyer stumbled. He looked at his younger sister. She grinned broadly and took the other man's hand and whirled away. Sawyer looked at her again across the lawn dance area. She wasn't little Stelcie any more. She was different now, no longer his little brat sister. She was grown up, or almost so. He stood there for a few moments, amazed at his discovery. "Things change," he said under his breath as he moved out of the other dancing couples' way.

He saw an old friend of his father's and walked over to talk with him. As he talked, he kept Stelcie in his vision for a time. At one point his eyes strayed to Miriam and followed her until the music stopped. Another young man approached her, and she danced with him when the music began again. Once, when they danced close near him, he saw Miriam smile his way.

Miriam smiled until she turned and saw another couple just arriving. The woman she did not know. Her escort was Solomon. Miriam's step hesitated slightly, but she put another smile on her face and at the next break in the music excused herself from her partner to seek her uncle and aunt, whom she found talking to the Dundees and the man they called Whitmore. She walked up and was promptly introduced to Mr. Whitmore as one of the two birthday celebrants.

Stelcie abruptly appeared at Miriam's side and immediately pointed at the refreshment table, saying, "There's Solomon and Miss Whitmore. Let's go talk."

"Oh, yes, let's do."

Miriam and Stelcie walked over, and Solomon introduced Eve Whitmore. He acquired a drink for each and pointed out to Miriam that rain was out of the question and that the present clouds would make a beautiful sunset. After some conversation about the lovely outdoor party decorations that had been strung through the trees and wooden archways and the gazebo, Solomon asked Eve to dance; and they excused themselves from the girls.

"Your cousin is quite handsome, Stelcie," said Miriam. "I've never met someone like him. There's something about him that just makes me gush when he looks at me. I hope I don't appear too, too foolish when I am in his presence." Miriam watched Eve and Solomon dance. She turned back to look at Stelcie and spotted a loose thread at Stelcie's waist on the right side. Miriam reached for it and tugged gently. The thread pulled free of the bunched red fabric, and Miriam held it up for Stelcie's examination. "A bit of red string for your thoughts." She dropped the red string, and it fluttered, twisting its way almost to the ground. Just before it snagged on a long blade

61

of grass, a sudden gust of wind lifted it high in the air and whipped it toward the river.

"Oh, it's jist a bit of red thread," remarked Stelcie, as she watched it flutter upward and away. "I . . . ."

"Miriam, may I have this dance?" asked a voice. She turned and saw Sawyer.

"Why, yes, Sawyer," she said with a smile. "I'd love to dance with you. Excuse us, will you, Stelcie?"

Miriam took Sawyer's hand and followed him into the flow of the dancing couples. Stelcie lost sight of them when a young man asked to dance with her.

At the corner of the house Mr. Surget, Mr. Dundee, Mr. Whitmore, and several other dignified older men grouped. Mr. Surget began introducing the group to Whitmore. "Let's see, Samuel, there are several gentlemen yew should become acquainted with. This is John Reposo. He and William Gustin here are from the Mississippi side of the river. They have cotton plantations here. This is Jarred Dayton. He raises cotton on the Louisiana side. Benjamin Davies and Henry Rowley. From Louisiana. Here is Richard Minorca, from this side. A cotton broker and grower." Each man shook hands with Samuel Whitmore as the introductions continued. "Clayton Cartwright is from across the river, too. William Barnard, J. B. Nevin. And Louis Stokman. All three from this side of the river. And here comes one of Natchez's bankers. Come over here, Bob. Meet Samuel Whitmore, from New Orleans. This is Robert J. Baxter, III."

Mr. Baxter said, "I know Mr. Whitmore, Frank. He came by the bank with a draft from New Orleans and opened an account." He shook Samuel's hand.

"Jist what are yew interested in here in Natchez?" asked John Reposo.

"A number of business opportunities, but especially land for cotton."

"We have some of the richest delta land in the South for raising cotton," said Henry Rowley.

"Are yew interested in living here?" William Barnard inquired.

"I just might be willing to relocate here in Natchez," answered Mr. Whitmore.

Across the way Sawyer, Solomon, and Eve Whitmore were talking with a riverboat captain and an older man named Holcumb, who had been a resident of Natchez for sixty years. He had a freight business under the hill for many of those years. They were discussing the history of Natchez and the Trace, the old path stretching northward to Nashville.

Mr. Holcumb said, "It wuz a lawless time back when I wuz a boy here. But it wuz tamer than afore the United States took over these territories. The Trace wuz full of outlaws. There wuz John Ford, one of the robbers who wuz noted fer his cruelty. Story be that a slave offended him; and in retaliation Ford puts his head in sum sort of a vise contraption and burnt out his eyes, tongue, and nose off. Heck, he be said to poisoned a friend of his so as to marry the friend's widow. Hearsay says that when he wuz to be put in the ground, the Devil's hand come up out of the grave to drag Ford's coffin straight down to Hell itself."

"Scary man," said Eve.

"Why, there's the legend of John Murrell, the preaching outlaw of the Natchez Trace and the territory over yonder to the Louisiana side. It's said he stole frum the French, the Spanish, and the Americans. But he preached hellfire and damnation and is said to have saved souls at camp meetings on both sides of the river. He wuz called 'the man in the Bolivar coat.' He done stole huge sums of money, gold and silver pieces. And slaves. Some say he plotted a conspiracy to start a slave uprising Christmas Day in 1835 that would begin right here in Natchez."

"Whatever happened to him?" asked Eve.

"Why, young lady, I don't rightly know what happened to old Murrell. Some folks says the Devil showed up at one camp meeting and snatched him away to eternal fire. Others say he jist got old and disappeared."

"What about the money, the treasure?" asked Solomon.

"He buried most of it, they say. Some people claim they found some. But there's only one man I believe ever found some of it. And yew know why I believe him?" Mr. Holcumb reached into his pocket and pulled out a silver coin. "This. This here is why. It's a Spanish silver piece. That's King Phillip there on one side. Look for yurself," he said as he handed the coin to Solomon, who handled the coin carefully and clasped it in his palm, feeling a warm sensation as he held it. He opened his hand, looked intently at the likeness of King Phillip, and then handed it to the riverboat captain. The captain held the coin between his fingers and offered it to Eve, whose fingers delicately took it to hold for a moment.

"It be my good luck piece," said Holcumb. "I kept it fer thirty years now."

"Did the man who gave you this say where it had been buried?" asked Solomon.

"He said . . . Let me try to remember. I think it wuz somewhere in Louisiana. In the area where them Frenchmen's settlements first start. A little south of the Red River. He had taken a steamer up to the first large town on the river and then he went . . . I, I can't remember that fur back," Holcumb stated.

"Let me see it again," said Solomon. He held the coin, feeling a strange affinity to it. It once more warmed his palm. He reluctantly handed it back to Holcumb.

"Yew interested in hunting some of John Murrell's buried treasure, boy?" asked Holcumb. "One piece of his silver may be lucky, but my friend who give me this here one had the ill fortune of having too many pieces of ill-gotten silver. He died slowly and painfully of a mad dog bite. He foamed at the mouth and went stark raving mad, they say."

"That's horrible," said Eve. "It makes me shiver."

"It's all right, little lady," said Holcumb. "At least he ain't died poor." Old man Holcumb cackled out a strange laugh.

"Dance with me, Solomon," implored Eve as she tugged at his arm.

Eve and Solomon left old Holcumb and the captain still talking as they went toward the musicians.

"You don't believe the old man, do you, Solomon?" asked Eve as they walked.

"Yes, Eve. I think I do," stated Solomon as he clenched his hand that had held the silver coin. "I think I do." He did not tell Eve that Holcumb's story of buried money reminded him of his Uncle Jeremiah's account of the Natchez Indians, fleeing Spanish soldiers, burying treasure at the Troyville Indian Mounds about thirty miles from Natchez.

A few dances later found Stelcie with her new friend Eli, Sawyer, Solomon, and Eve sitting and talking beneath one of the large magnolia trees.

"We hope you remain in Natchez, Eve," said Stelcie. "We can be grand friends, yew and Miriam and me."

65

"I hope we remain, too," Eve said, her eyes feasting on Solomon's smile. Out of the corner of his eye, Solomon noticed Miriam approaching.

"My dear Miriam. How callous of me. I have yet to dance with you, the other birthday girl. Shall we now?" said Solomon. "You will pardon us, won't you, Eve?"

"Yes, of course," Eve said perfunctorily. Her eyes followed the couple.

Sawyer asked, "Why sit here? Eve, let's dance, too."

Eve stood and took Sawyer's arm. Stelcie and her friend got up to dance, also.

While dancing with Sawyer, Eve could hardly keep her eyes off Solomon and Miriam. She answered Sawyer's questions about her New Orleans home and upbringing politely but tersely. As the music ended, she heard her father call her name and motion to her. "Father is calling me. Excuse me, Sawyer."

"Of course."

Mr. Whitmore took Eve over to be introduced to several people, men and women, and she became caught up in a whirl of introductions, questions, and conversation.

In the meantime, Solomon, seeing that Eve was occupied with meeting new people, suggested to Miriam that they get away from the music and the others briefly to talk.

"But Eve is—"

"Eve is with her father, meeting people. I'll be alone for a time. Let's go into the garden there for a few minutes, to talk quietly. No one will miss us," he added confidently.

"How can I resist your charm?" Miriam said as he held out his hand to her. They walked silently for a time to a spot behind a trellis;

and there, out of sight of the others, Solomon took Miriam in his arms and kissed her passionately. At first, unsure of herself, Miriam was hesitant to return the feeling, but she could not resist Solomon's fiery embrace. The heat of the moment consumed her, and she lost control. Solomon Witcher was all that existed—no Eve, no party full of friends, no aunt and uncle, no Clifton. There was only Solomon.

He ended the kiss, but her lips followed his until he stood straight. Then she looked up into his shadowy face. "Solomon, I . . . I—"

"Shh. Don't say anything," he quickly whispered. "We must get back to the party. Before you are missed." Smiling sweetly at her, he put a finger on her lips and gently pressed. Then he put his hands on her shoulders and gave her a wistful look. Before she knew it, he had ushered her back along the same path that they had used to leave the party. They approached the edge of the shadows, and Solomon turned slightly to say, "Wait here a moment. I'll go on." Miriam obeyed meekly while he strode quickly back into the light and sound and blended into the figures moving about. She sighed heavily, feeling weak-kneed and almost trembling, rooted in place. Thoughts of Solomon swirled in her consciousness.

She heard voices behind her. She turned about quickly. The voices were closer. Regaining her composure, she moved back into the swell of the party, turning to see who was approaching on the path from the same direction. A couple emerged from the shadows. It was Stelcie and that young man named Eli. She wondered if they had been close and had seen Solomon with her.

"Miriam. Miriam," called Charlotte Surget. Miriam turned toward her aunt's voice.

"Yes, ma'am."

"Find Stelcie and tell her to come over to the table over yonder. Yew, too. It's time for the cake," she said.

"Yes, ma'am."

Miriam looked about for Stelcie. She saw her and headed her way. "Stelcie, come over here, girl. They'll be bringing cake out. Aunt Charlotte wants us at that table. Come on," Miriam said as she grabbed Stelcie's hand and pulled her away from her companion. Eli followed, but he was not expecting the quick pace Miriam used and fell a few steps behind at first.

"What's your hurry, dear Miriam?" asked Stelcie.

"Did you see, while you and Eli were walking? Did you see?" Miriam kept walking. "Oh, never you mind me."

"Did I see what?"

"Never you mind. Don't listen to my babbling. I'm excited about all this."

"And Solomon, too," giggled Stelcie.

"What?"

"Over here, girls," said Mr. Surget. "Come over here." He motioned to them. "Everyone. Everyone," he boomed out in a louder voice. The musicians, who had been alerted to the activity forthcoming, abruptly stopped playing. "Everyone. Everyone! Come over here! Party guests and dear friends," he continued as the people began to crowd around him, his wife, the Dundees, and the girls. "The Dundees and Charlotte and I invited y'all to this party to help us celebrate the birthdays of Stelcie Dundee and Miriam Surget, my niece. These young ladies are practically grown, and we want to take note of that and tell them how much we love them. Happy birthday, Stelcie and Miriam!"

At these words a huge three-layer cake about five feet in length and two feet wide was brought out on a table. Stelcie's name was on one end, and Miriam's was on the other. "Happy Birthday" in giant letters was in the middle, ringed by burning candles.

The crowd began shouting "happy birthday" to both young celebrants with some guests approaching to embrace them.

Jeremiah Dundee said to the two when he hugged and kissed each, "Yore gifts are inside in the room opening to this terrace. After yew finish here, why not go in with yore friends to open the presents?"

Moving with the crowd, Eve and Solomon edged closer and closer toward Stelcie and Miriam. They reached Stelcie first and congratulated her with hugs and kisses. Then they moved to Miriam. Eve politely but warmly grasped Miriam's hands and then kissed her on the side of the face. Solomon did likewise, but his kiss on the side of her face left it burning. "Happy birthday," he said.

"Thank you," Miriam replied weakly as Eve and Solomon moved on so that others could extend their congratulations and well wishes.

Solomon and Eve moved away from the crowd of people and walked toward the same dark path that he earlier had walked with Miriam. "Where are we going?" asked Eve.

"Away from the others for a time. To a quiet place where we can talk," he replied.

Eve grasped his arm and let him lead her along. They walked to and past the spot where Solomon had kissed Miriam. "Come along," whispered Solomon.

They walked to the bluff overlooking the Mississippi River. The moon was alone in the cloudless night sky.

"Eve, I hope you and your father choose to reside in Natchez," he said softly as they stopped on the highest point of the bluff overlooking the Mississippi River. He slipped his arms around her and smiled at her.

"I hope father can find what he's seeking," she responded. "I want to stay, too." She closed her eyes.

Solomon pulled her closer and kissed her softly. She responded warmly. His lips lingered on hers. As he pulled back, they both looked out over the river.

"It's beautiful," Eve said.

"Yes."

"And Clifton is, too," added Eve.

"I agree. One day I'll have something like this. I'll have an estate," said Solomon.

"Solomon, I think we should get back."

"You're right," he said after a moment or two. He kissed her again, and then they started on their way back to the party.

In a few minutes they had rejoined the others. They danced and talked and laughed the remainder of the time.

Back at the Silver Street Hotel, he walked the Whitmores inside, exchanged well-wishes, and went back into the night.

Several weeks passed, reacquainting Natchez with the hot afternoon sun and high temperatures of August. Little rain had fallen since the party. Heat was a big problem for everyone.

Sawyer was at the saw mill, helping with the sawing of board lumber since the early morning. Solomon was out riding with an employee, inspecting the cotton fields on the newest section of acquired land. Jeremiah was at a timber cut northeast of Natchez.

The afternoon was hotter than usual. Only a few thin, wispy clouds were in the distant eastern sky. Sawyer had just paused to wipe the sweat from his forehead with his blue bandana when he saw a wagon load of logs being driven in. As the wagon approached, he recognized the two men on it: Jeremiah and Ezra, a free black man. Their voices were almost audible despite the distance, old Ezra gesticulating awkwardly as he steered closer. As the wagon came closer, Sawyer stepped down from his work platform and peered intently at the two men on the wagon. He heard both Ezra and his father loudly impatient with one another.

"They're arguing about something," said Sawyer to himself.

The wagon pulled to a stop. Sawyer walked up to it and now could hear what the men were saying.

"But Mr. Dundee, yew been dizzy-like and pale like de ghosts. Mister needs to see de doctor," argued Ezra.

"Old Ezra, what do yew know. I jist got too hot. I'll rest a spell. I'll be all right. Stop yore nagging." Jeremiah sat still. He didn't jump down quickly from the wagon as he usually did.

"What's the matter, Daddy?"

"Oh, nothing," he said faintly and then went silent.

Ezra quickly said, "Mister Dundee here done gots too hot while achoppin' pine trees. He done some staggerin' likes he be drunk. He be stubborn. He won't slow down." Ezra pointed to Jeremiah's face and said, "See Mister's pale white face, Massa Saw. Yew see. We'ns done tole him to see de doctor. But he don't wants to lissen."

"Get down, Daddy," said Sawyer with a concerned look on his face as he reached his hand up to his father. "Come down off the wagon. Let's get a drink. I need one."

Jeremiah rose from the seat to climb down. He stood straight and cast a shadow over Sawyer. As he moved a foot forward, he swayed and then grasped his left shoulder with his right hand. Words now took effort. "Saw." He looked down at Sawyer, saying in a low gutteral tone, "Saw, git Laura fer me." He gasped for a breath and toppled off the wagon into his son's arms, causing father and son to fall heavily onto the dusty ground.

Ezra shouted, "Hep! Hep! Mister Dundee needs hep!"

Workers streamed to the Dundees and assisted Sawyer in carrying his father over to the shade of a tree and in leaning his upper body against the trunk. Ezra removed his shirt, placing it to cushion Jeremiah's head. Jeremiah, still clutching his left shoulder, struggled to breathe and let out a low pitiful moan each time he exhaled. He began to sweat even more profusely.

Sawyer sent one worker to fetch Doctor Whiddon from town. Another was sent to get Laura Dundee. Jeremiah's shirt was loosened, and a wet cloth was given to Sawyer to wipe his father's face.

"Hold on, Daddy, hold on," said Sawyer desperately. "Doc Whiddon will be here. We sent for Mama."

Jeremiah said nothing. He merely stared outwardly and blankly. His face had a grim expression; his breathing was still labored; and now his body jerked involuntarily causing his arms to flail weakly. His mouth emitted froth that gushed down over his chin and onto his body. He suddenly became still once again. He continued to stare outward into the distance.

Sawyer prayed aloud as he continued to dab the sweat away from his father's ashen face. His father's shallow breathing and almost imperceptible moans worried him and reinforced his worst fears. Twenty minutes passed. Thirty. Nothing changed. The workers milled about, talking in low tones.

Everyone could hear the noise of galloping horses pulling a light wagon approaching. Gabriel drove the horses into the mill yard, and Sawyer saw Laura and Stelcie in the wagon. As soon as the horses were halted, Gabriel hurriedly jumped from the driver's seat to help Laura down.

Mrs. Dundee, tears flowing down her face, cried out, "Jeremiah! Jeremiah!"

"Daddy! Daddy!" exclaimed Stelcie, leaping down from the wagon.

Sobbing, Laura rushed to her husband and cradled his head in her hands.

Jeremiah feebly raised his head to look at his wife. Anguish and pain showed on his face. His lips moved to form a word. He winced and used his right arm to reach to his left shoulder. "Laura," he said. He smiled weakly at his wife. His body shook once again. His mouth foamed excessively now. His eyes closed, and he was still.

"Oh, my God!" shouted Laura. She lifted his head and shoulders to her breast and wept openly as Stelcie let out a cry of anguish.

"Daddy. Daddy," exclaimed Stelcie.

Sawyer sat backwards on the ground. Tears clouded in his eyes and swarmed down his face. "No," he said hoarsely.

Horse's hooves were heard again. Now a buggy hurried into the yard. Dr. Whiddon jumped out, clutching his black bag. He moved quickly to Jeremiah Dundee and looked him over.

Sawyer now moved to his mother and tugged her into an embrace and pulled Stelcie to them both.

Laura Dundee asked quietly, "Has someone gone for Solomon?"

"No," answered Sawyer. He turned to one of the men. "Henry, go to the new cotton acreage past the Normand house. Tell Solomon to come home right away."

"Yus, sur, boss."

The wagon ride back to the Dundee home site was long and solemn. Stelcie cried all the way. Laura, weeping profusely, sat on the floor of the wagon by her husband's body.

As they turned off the main road to reach the house, they could see Beulah and the other slaves at the home site gathering outside. Beulah ran to the wagon and started shouting, "Oh, Jesus! Sweet Jesus!" She wailed loudly. The others crowded around the wagon in stunned silence for a while. Then the weeping began.

Jeremiah Dundee's body was placed on a table in the front parlor where he had always talked with his friends and guests. The undertaker was sent for, and other arrangements were pondered.

Two days later, Jeremiah Dundee was buried near his mother atop a hill overlooking the Dundee homestead. As the last strains of "Amazing Grace" echoed around them, the mourners began to trickle away. Laura Dundee turned sharply away as the coffin was lowered. She took two steps, stopped, and turned to look back at Sawyer, who was still standing in the same spot he had been.

As the gathering dispersed, Solomon and Stelcie held one another, slowly walking behind the crowd. The Surgets, the Whitmores, and other friends of the Dundees were now moving down the slope.

"Saw, come on. Bless his heart. He's gone," Laura said quietly. "Saw."

Sawyer turned. A single tear trickled down his cheek. He took a step, then another to be next to her. His mother latched herself to his arm. "I knew he would die at that sawmill," she said mournfully. They walked on down the hill to let the gravediggers finish their work.

Monday morning found the Dundees and Solomon in the law office of Franklin H. Whittington. Laura and Stelcie sat on a sofa in the large office. Solomon and Sawyer sat on wooden straight-back chairs directly in front of lawyer Whittington's desk.

Mr. Whittington began, "Jeremiah Dundee, my long-time friend, had written a will several years ago, long before you young men went away to school in the north. Quite recently—in fact, in a conversation at the party at Clifton—Jeremiah mentioned to me that he wished to amend his will in the near future. Unfortunately, he had not come in to this office to make the changes that he had in mind. Therefore, we are bound by what is contained in this document I have in hand. I assure y'all that everything is in proper legal order and standing." At this point Mr. Whittington paused. He then read, "I, Jeremiah Albert Dundee, being of sound mind and by my own hand of my own free will make the following bequests with my estate: To my loving wife Laura, I leave the Dundee homestead, the house servants, and one quarter-interest in the sawmill. To my daughter Stelcie, I leave the sum of $500 to be given at the time of her marriage and one-quarter interest in the sawmill. To my beloved nephew Solomon, I leave the sum of $500 to be given immediately for investment purposes and the right of occupancy in the Dundee homestead as long as he shall live. To my son Sawyer, I leave one-half interest in the sawmill, all land, buildings, animals, and slaves associated with it, with the exception of the homestead itself and its servants (which are assigned to Laura Dundee), and all other investments and financial accounts under my name at the time of my demise. All the above is conditional upon the agreement of Laura Dundee, Stelcie Dundee, and Sawyer Dundee to free all persons that are Dundee slaves at the end of three years from today's date. Also, it shall be announced publicly that Beulah is not a slave and has not

75

been a slave since January 1, 1850. Beulah's manumission papers and legal registration papers for Adams County and the State of Mississippi and payment of related fees are on file in the law office of F. H. Whittington and also can be found at the Dundee homestead. Signed: Jeremiah Albert Dundee. Witnessed by Franklin H. Whittington, R. M. Watson, and Paul J. Wilson."

They sat in silence for a time. Mr. Whittington was the one to speak again. "Sawyer, you are quite well off. I can show you the listing of your assets whenever you wish. Today or later."

He looked at Solomon. Opening a desk drawer, he took out a piece of paper and handed it to him. "This is a bank draft on your uncle's bank here in Natchez. Present it to Mr. Baxter any time." Solomon, silent, reached to take the paper.

Mr. Whittington looked at each person and then said, "I have nothing further. Do you have any questions?"

Stelcie asked, "Yew mean that Beulah is not a slave?"

"That is correct," Laura Dundee finally spoke up. "Beulah has not been a slave for about ten years now."

"Does she know?" asked Sawyer.

"Yes, she does," said Laura. "Jeremiah emancipated her back then, and she decided to remain with us at a monthly salary because she had nowhere else to go and no family of her own to take her in. She said that we were her family. We kept her status a secret for her protection and peace of mind. Jeremiah freed her because of something Beulah had done for yore Grandma Dundee in the past. Beulah never talks about it. What it was goes to the grave with yore father. Jeremiah even gave Grandma Dundee's Bible to Beulah unknown to all of yew. I was not privy to any of the reasons why."

"I do have all the legal papers, properly filed with county and state officials," added the lawyer. "Any other questions from any of you?"

There being none, the group left his office and returned home. Stelcie and Laura Dundee disappeared upstairs to cry another time. Sawyer and Solomon went to sit on the front porch.

A mass of gray clouds was approaching from the west. Thunder rumbled from the sky. The whole day darkened.

Sawyer looked at Solomon, who was staring at the sycamine tree. "Daddy was going to amend his will for you, Solomon. I know that was what Mr. Whittington had mentioned," Sawyer said. "Don't feel bad. I can split most of what I received with you."

"No. No. I realize what you mean. I have no hard feelings toward Uncle Jeremiah. He and Aunt Laura raised me and took care of me. I wanted for nothing. I know I have a place here. You and I had plans to work into Uncle Jeremiah's business, and all of us could have done well together. But now things have changed."

"What do you mean, Solomon?"

"I mean that I have decided to seek my fortune with the money Uncle Jeremiah left me. I'll be leaving in a few days. I have some personal business to take care of and some people to say goodbye to for a time."

"Solomon, don't leave us."

"I must. Now that things have changed; this is the time. Remember the party and the old man with the silver coin and the story of John Murrell, the outlaw? Well, Saw, I think I can find some of that buried money. I had the feeling ever since I held the Spanish silver coin in my palm. I know I can find some of it. You know how I get these feelings—about cards and winning."

"Solomon, if it's money you want . . . "

"No, it's not just money. This is something I must do. I'm going to talk with old man Holcumb again. I'll tell Aunt Laura and Stelcie tonight. You can't talk me out of it. I've decided. I won't change my mind. Don't worry. I'll be back as soon as I find what I'm looking for. You know I'll do just as I say. See that sycamine. Remember Grandma Dundee and faith? I have it. I'll find some of Murrell's buried silver."

They both looked at the sycamine tree. The wind gusted, shaking the leaves violently. Raindrops pelted the tree and everything else. Lightning flashed in the sky, and the thunder cracked in the dark clouds.

The next day found Solomon knocking at the door of old man Holcumb. "Hello, Mr. Holcumb. How are you this day?"

"I ain't feeling the best today, but I'll make it. Yew're that Witcher boy. From the party at Clifton. Ain't yew?"

"Yes, Mr. Holcumb, you're right. It's Solomon Witcher. My uncle is, er, was Jeremiah Dundee."

"Come in, boy," said old Mr. Holcumb. "Come on in. Sorry 'bout Jeremiah." Holcumb opened the door wide and motioned Solomon inside. "Set a spell. What brings yew to see me?" Holcumb sat on one of the chairs in the parlor of his house. Solomon sat on the sofa.

"Mr. Holcumb, I don't know exactly how to ask you what I need to ask you," said Solomon.

Holcumb looked at him in a perplexed way. "Speak up, boy."

"Well, Mr. Holcumb, I am fascinated by your story of John Murrell, the outlaw. Actually, it's the buried silver and gold. I'm leaving soon to seek my fortune. My late uncle left me a substantial amount of money, but for what I want to do it is not adequate. I must have more capital."

"What does all that have to do with me? I tole yew all I kin remember of what my friend tole me. I ain't remembering much better these days. All I can do is say agin what I done said."

"Yes. That will help me. I'll need you to repeat some things, but that's not what I need the most from you, Mr. Holcumb," stated Solomon.

"Well, boy, what?"

"That silver piece. That coin."

"Yew need my good luck piece?" Holcumb looked at Solomon Witcher in disbelief. "Do yew know what yew're askin'?"

"Yes," said Solomon intently, looking directly into Holcumb's eyes. "I know I want to buy it from you. How much do you want for it?"

"Boy, the silver piece is more than jist a coin, a possession. It's special. Yew know that."

"Yes, I know," said Solomon with a certain determination in his voice. "I'll give you $200 for it."

"No. It ain't fer sale."

"Mr. Holcumb," said Solomon, standing and still looking the old man dead in the eyes. "I'll make it $500."

"It ain't the money, boy."

Solomon's voice lowered, and he smiled wantonly. "Holcumb, I want that silver piece. I need it to find more of John Murrell's hidden money. I will have it." He glared at old Holcumb.

Old man Holcumb was mesmerized by the look that Solomon gave him. Holcumb stared blankly at Solomon.

"Holcumb, I must have that silver piece. With it in my possession I will find some of the outlaw's buried treasure. I will have it from you. I will have it from you now," said Solomon in a demanding tone.

"But Witcher," uttered the old man.

"I will have it!" exclaimed Solomon.

The old man stood, his breathing labored, and stared at Solomon. Solomon didn't blink an eye. Old man Holcumb trembled and sat back on his chair. Solomon's intense look bewitched the old man.

"But, Witcher, will I git my lucky piece back?"

Solomon, in a firm but reassuring voice, replied, "Of course, Mr. Holcumb, I will return your lucky silver piece as soon as I locate some of Murrell's hidden treasure. I'll keep your silver coin in a secure place on my person. Whatever happens to your silver coin happens to me."

"A promise?"

"A promise," Solomon replied, smiling saintly, as he held out his hand for the old man to put the silver coin into. "I swear it." Solomon now asked for Holcumb to relate the story of the coin once more.

The old man repeated the information about the outlaw and where he heard the silver coin had been found. As he stood, Holcumb reached into his vest pocket and retrieved the silver coin. He carefully placed it into Solomon Witcher's palm.

"Thank you, Mr. Holcumb. The next time I see you, I'll be a very rich man." Solomon grinned broadly and left the house without giving him any money.

Old Holcumb turned slightly, watched Solomon leave and the door close behind him, and pondered on what had just happened. "How did that boy talk me out of my lucky piece?" he asked himself in disbelief. "And no money." Holcumb dropped himself into the nearest chair, "Oh, my head aches!"

Solomon next called on the Surgets at Clifton to explain what he was planning to do. Miriam and Solomon talked for an hour about his proposed adventure after Mrs. Surget left them alone. Miriam followed him out of the front of the house to where his horse waited. He grasped her hand, lifted it, and kissed it lightly. His eyes riveted to hers as he said, "I'll be back as soon as I can, Miriam. You'll be here, won't you?"

"Yes. I won't leave until I hear from you. I'll wait," she replied.

"Good."

With that word, he mounted his horse Midnight and trotted away, not turning in the saddle to look back. Miriam raised her hand and waved.

Back in Natchez itself, Solomon called at the Whitmore's house. It was a neat two-story building with a front porch. The black maid Cryer answered the door, invited Solomon in, and went to inform Eve of her company.

"Solomon, how nice to see you," said Eve, smiling warmly.

"You may not be too happy with what I'm going to say," he said, grasping her hand while offering a boyish smile of reassurance.

"What?"

Solomon related his plans to Eve. "Why?" she asked several times on the verge of tears. The last time he showed her the silver piece he had acquired from old Holcumb.

81

"I'll be back as soon as I can," he promised, holding her hands in his. He embraced her before he left.

The next day, after a tearful farewell at the Dundee homestead, Solomon Witcher rode off toward Natchez on Midnight to catch the ferry to cross the Mississippi River to Vidalia, Louisiana, to find gold and silver hidden by the legendary outlaw-preacher John Murrell. As he rode out by the sycamine tree, he turned to look at it a moment longer and remembered Grandma Dundee's words.

He thought about all Grandma Dundee had said to him when no one else was around to hear. Most of what he now remembered had been told to him late at night when the weather was stormy and frightening to him as a little boy. What Grandma Dundee told him was scary at first, but after several years transformed from scary to unbelievable to compelling at each revelation of information from his old grandma. There was the caul that Grandma Dundee said came from his birthing. He had it in a small metal box that she had owned. He had looked at what appeared to be some dried skin or membrane in the box, but he couldn't distinguish exactly what it was. He knew the metal box was her prized possession she had brought across the ocean from her birthplace in Scotland. He knew that it must be important because Grandma Dundee had saved it and had given the metal box to him the night of her seventy-seventh birthday just before she died at sun rise, along with the words, "Yew will never drown whilst yew possess this caul. Keep it, boy. It will make yew have a way with words that other men do not." He remembered the old woman's claw of a hand touching his face while she reiterated, "Listen to me, the Dundee sithcundman." Her fingers were icy on his face, but her words, even though somewhat eerie, were strangely warming to his soul. Much of what she told him he kept in his heart, unsure of its purposes.

Beulah, watching him from the house, saw him looking at the sycamine and said in a low voice that no one else could hear, "Dat

82

Solomon be spooky. I wonders 'bout him whens he gits back."
Beulah, too, remembered some of the late-night conversations
overheard between Grandma Dundee and Solomon.

Across the river Solomon led Midnight off the ferry, mounted
him, looked back at Natchez under the hill and above the hill, and then
urged his horse onward. Solomon did not know exactly where he was
going. He thought that he would sense when he was near what he
sought. Old Holcumb's Spanish silver piece he had put in a small
pouch hanging from his neck by a leather string. He placed his hand
on top of it now and thought of Grandma Dundee. The small metal
box she had given him was at the bottom of his saddlebag. Midnight
walked on.

Troyville (Jonesville), Louisiana

Solomon thought he would go to the Troyville Indian Mounds near the confluence of the Little, Tensas, Ouachita, and Black Rivers. He remembered Uncle Jeremiah once taking Sawyer and him to see the mounds while he was scouting timber in the area. He thought it would be about a thirty-mile journey. He was in no hurry at the moment to seek his fortune. He knew he would have some sort of inner guidance for his quest. His thoughts would have to simmer within his brain for a time.

Solomon crossed Black River on the ferry at the settlement by the mounds. He thought about the trip to the mounds with his uncle and his cousin, his personal encounter with that large canebrake rattlesnake, and the story his uncle told about the possible hidden treasure there. His uncle had related the legend that the Natchez Indians were running from and attempting to escape the Spaniards years and years ago. The Natchez Indians had carried their silver and gold treasures with them but were afraid that the Spaniards were about to overrun them and capture their precious treasures. According to the legend, the Natchez Tribe buried their valuables somewhere near the Troyville Indian Mounds and then escaped their tormentors. Solomon wondered if he was destined to find the buried wealth of the Natchez Indians. He would walk the area, climb the mounds, and try to maintain a meditative state of mind in the hope that he'd feel the familiar sort of inner guidance that so often seemed to steer him to good fortune. He decided to sleep on the first open mound or raised area not near a house. As night fell, he found a good spot to stake Midnight and bed down. He lay there in his blanket, looking up at the beautiful night sky full of bright stars. He felt very small for a time; but as sleep began to overtake him, that sense of insignificance was replaced by the familiar positive feeling of favorable fortune. He fell asleep. That night he dreamed of the Spaniards chasing the Natchez Indians and shooting and killing many of them. Suddenly in his dream he felt himself thrust into the role of a Spanish soldier. He became an active participant in his dream, even though he was unaware of the situation being that of a dream. He chased one of the Indians who was moving more slowly than the others. He pasted his eyes on this single warrior. The reason for his slowness was that he was carrying some fully-loaded bags. They appeared to be heavy. His eye followed the individual in the distance among the trees leading up to one of the mounds. Other Spanish soldiers fired weapons, killing many of the Indians. But he watched that one warrior closely. The Indian ducked in among a thicket of trees as his fellow tribesmen continued to run toward the mound. Thinking no one had observed him, the Indian crouched among the thick trees, but Solomon slowed his gait and watched the Indian. The Indian now dug furiously with his weapon. Solomon stopped just to watch. The warrior had a fairly deep hole now and pushed three bags into it. He began to put dirt back in the hole on top of the bags. Solomon moved forward toward the thicket. Other Indians and soldiers had passed the thicket several minutes ago, and gunshots could be heard up and on the near mound. Gathering leaves and branches quickly, the Indian covered his digging area. Solomon now was at the thicket and moved between the trees, raising his weapon to fire directly at the warrior. Seeing Solomon at the same time, the Indian rushed toward him swinging his club and gesturing with his knife. Solomon pulled the trigger on his musket. Instead of the loud noise of the discharging gun, he heard nothing but the scream of the warrior. The Indian raised his club, and Solomon watched it arc downward toward his face. He felt a warm sensation on his forehead.

The hot sun rays struck Solomon directly on his forehead. Their warmth awakened him. He had cold sweat upon his entire face, even though the wind was gusting in spurts. "What a dream!" he thought to himself. He ran his right hand over his face to wipe the sweat. He sat upright and reached for his hat.

85

The frightening dream served as a push to make Solomon think more about the fact he needed to seek his fortune, to fulfill his dreams of owning a mansion like Clifton with much land and hundreds of slaves. He was going to be one of the elite in Natchez and its surrounding area on both sides of the Mississippi River. He knew that he was going to be important. It was his destiny. It was meant to be.

Solomon led Midnight across open ground and up and down the smaller elevated groundswells in the area. By early afternoon he had stood at the top of each of the lesser earthworks. Canebrakes covered most of the area, including the tops and sides of some of the mounds. On each mound or what was left of one he stood at the highest point he could in spite of the heavy canebrakes and looked to the east and then the west. He had concentrated on his inner feelings and rubbed old man Holcumb's coin in the pouch hanging from his neck. He felt nothing unusual, no special sense of direction. He had no premonition about buried treasure. He had saved the largest mound, the highest elevation, until last to climb. Its tallest point seemed to be about fifty feet from the regular ground level.

He had not mounted Midnight the entire day; he had held reins and pulled the horse along with him. The horse nibbled at tufts of grass every time they stopped for Solomon to think and meditate. "You must be wondering what the heck I am doing today, aren't you, boy?" Solomon said to Midnight. The horse looked at him quizzically and shook his head up and down and sideways, too. "Yeah, I am not sure of what I am doing either." The wind started gusting again from the southeast and almost pushed Solomon's hat off his head. He repositioned his hat and pulled it down tighter on his head. He pulled Midnight up the last big mound as he ascended the steep incline.

The view was spectacular from the side next to the rivers. The sky was a beautiful light blue, and there were a few puffy white clouds slowly sailing from the southwest to the northeast. Solomon could see far in the distance toward Natchez. He wondered how far away Natchez was in terms of how the proverbial crow flies. He took a step to the side. The surface was uneven, probably from excavations to remove dirt and to hunt for buried valuables. He thought he must stand on the highest point on this largest mound the way he had stood on the highest point of the lesser mounds. The wind turned into stronger gusts from the southwest. Each gust of cool wind gave Solomon a pleasant feeling across his face and head. He made his way to the highest ground on the mound. Solomon let go of Midnight's reins, knowing the horse would not go far from him.

Solomon, standing there and looking out at the view of the rivers' confluence, imagined what this specific point of the Indian mounds was like in its height of power and influence. His uncle had told Sawyer and him that the old people on the Louisiana side of the Mississippi River told tales of a village of power and influence that had been on this site. There were several mounds, and on one was an additional mound with a conical or pyramid-like tower built on the second mound. Since this site was a village directly on the river, trade flourished at this confluence of four rivers. Solomon envisioned that grand ceremonies with elaborate rituals were conducted here. He felt a connection with those peoples. His Grandma Dundee often said that the family had Indian blood in their veins. If there was truth to what Grandma Dundee had said, perhaps he had an ancestor who was a shaman. A sudden gust of wind disturbed his thinking and brought him back to reality. He thought that he should take a few steps to reach a higher surface.

At the highest point of the mound, Solomon turned his focus inward. He stood still for a few moments as he looked to the east from whence he had come. He turned about and stared toward the west—the direction he was to go. The wind gusted enough to cause him to break his focus and turn his attention to maintaining his balance. The wind swirled and changed direction. At this moment Midnight whinnied loudly, causing Solomon to turn to look at him. Solomon's attention now focused on his horse a bit upwind of him. As Solomon looked at Midnight, a strong gust of wind carried a bright red bit of string in front of his face. The wind swirled again, twirling the red string about in the air, and then whisked it away upward and out of sight. The gusty wind tamed itself, leaving Solomon looking out over the water and pondering the whirling dervish of red string.

Alexandria, Louisiana

Solomon left Troyville the next morning after a dreamless sleep. For several days Solomon rode slowly, looking at the nature's scenery and waiting patiently for a feeling as he touched ever so often the pouch holding the coin. He was heading northwestward. Now he turned southward, thinking to look along the banks of the Red River. In Alexandria, after crossing the river, he spent two nights, playing cards each night and winning a little money and the favor of several of the ladies working the tavern.

Solomon spent several days following the Red River upstream in a general northwesterly direction. He became dissatisfied with this direction, but he had to test it. He remembered that old Holcumb had mentioned Frenchmen. He knew that the nearest French settlements were southeast of Alexandria. But he wanted to test his "sense" of treasure-seeking. Within an hour after his turnabout he felt happier. He felt "on course." He reached Alexandria again. He spent several days and nights there, playing cards, drinking, and reveling in the attention of every woman he encountered.

One night he played poker with a Frenchman that won almost as many hands as did Solomon. Solomon struck up conversations among a series of hands in which the old Frenchman named Decuir was winning. Solomon questioned the man about the nearest French settlement close to the Red River. He was told that it was the Marksville area, but that Marksville was six or seven miles away from the river itself, and southeast of Alexandria. By mid-morning he was astride Midnight and on the trail. He anticipated getting to Marksville the next day before nightfall unless he wandered about looking longer than he thought he might. He knew that he wouldn't stick to the main trail. He had to search when the urge hit him. He still wondered what his sign would be, what would make him stop and decide where to dig. What was he looking for?

Marksville, Louisiana (and elsewhere in Avoyelles Parish)

He rode on. The sky darkened with the accumulation of black thunderclouds in the west behind him. The dark, heavy clouds advanced over and beyond him. The wind picked up. Strong gusts made him pull his hat on tighter and swayed the treetops. Lightning bolted down in jagged streaks with loud claps of thunder. Midnight became nervous. The periodic lightning and thunder startled mount and rider. The rain came down in sheets gusted sideways by the wind, large heavy drops that hurt Solomon's hands in a strange pleasing way.

The trail became one of mud and nothing else. The rain was so heavy that Solomon could hardly see the trail, and he simply gave Midnight a loose rein to walk along on his own.

It was night now, pitch black except for the occasional brilliant flashes of lightning. The storm seemed to sit above him. The low areas were flooding, and all of the earth was drenched; so it was no use to stop to camp. No outside fire could be started. Solomon traveled on, allowing his horse to pick his way.

About midnight a sheet of lightning flashed and illuminated the entire southeastern sky. Solomon thought he saw a house, a small house in the distance. He thought the people there, if any, may offer shelter for a time.

Suddenly there was a single jagged streak of lightning striking within twenty yards of Solomon and Midnight, followed immediately by an extremely loud boom of thunder. Midnight reared. Solomon, not holding onto the reins tightly and he himself caught unaware, was thrown from the slick, wet saddle.

The rain falling with force on his face and head awakened him. Midnight was standing close by, looking at him. Solomon unconsciously felt the back of his head. He couldn't tell if he was

90

bleeding or not in the darkness and rain. His head throbbed in the back and the front. He raised up but felt groggy. He stood, unsure of his footing. Slowly he took steps toward Midnight, whom he could barely see. The lightning lit up the night again. More thunder. Its booming made his head throb at the temples. The throbbing eased up, and Solomon began to get his bearings once more.

At the next lightning flash, Solomon saw the small house again. He had to get there. He reached for his horse and touched Midnight's rump. He used the horse to steady himself. He held the bridle strap beside the horse's head and started to lead the horse slowly toward the house. Solomon could see a dim light from a window. "Someone must be living there," he thought. His head was clearing as he got closer, but the throbbing in the back continued and even increased in strength. "I just need to get out of this storm," he said aloud to his horse. They made it to the front porch. Solomon patted Midnight on the withers and stumbled up the few steps. He heard loud, excited voices from within. He thought he heard a female voice crying out in pain. He pushed the door open and fell inward on his knees.

Inside the house, a woman screamed out, but not in fear of Solomon Witcher. She was crying out because she was in the last stages of childbirth. Her husband, holding her hand at the moment Solomon had burst in, and she had not expected an interloper during the storm.

Solomon was astonished at what he saw. He was breathing heavily, but not as deeply and heavily as the woman. She said something Solomon did not understand. So did the short, dark-tanned man. Solomon's mind was becoming clearer. He saw the immediacy of the situation. The husband spoke in French, but not the proper French Solomon had studied in a course in school. Solomon, in his condition with his head hurting and with the storm not abating at the moment, could only understand several of the words. What he heard was a Cajun dialect. Solomon, despite the throb of pain in his head, pieced together enough information to recognize that he had stumbled upon a French family. The Cajun man spoke nervously to Solomon, but Solomon did not understand.

The woman screamed out in pain once again. The Frenchman directed his attention back to his wife. Solomon sat back, pushed the door closed, and leaned against it. He closed his eyes and felt the tremendous pain in the back of his head. He put his hand there. He felt a warm wetness and looked at it. He saw blood through his blurry eyes. He closed his eyes to rest them. His whole body ached. He knew that the woman was delivering a baby, but he needed a few moments to himself, to revitalize after being out in the storm. His head ached with dull pulsing pain. He lost consciousness for a few seconds.

When he heard the excited voices of the man and woman again, he forced his eyes open. His eyes closed involuntarily. He knew something was alarming them. He jerked open his eyes and saw the woman crying and heard her speaking in terse, hurried phrases. The man held a baby. It was motionless and silent. The man cradled it and slapped its bottom. It appeared a strange shade of bloody blue in the flickering candlelight. Solomon thought his eyes were playing tricks on him because he could not clearly see the baby's face. He squinted and tried to re-focus his eyes. He still could not make out the face of the baby. The man cradled the baby and fell to his knees beside his wife's bed. He held the still infant up to his weakened wife, and both cried out in grief and despair.

Summoning all his strength, Solomon stood up and moved quickly over to the bed and took the baby from the astonished Frenchman's hands. He held it by its tiny chest with his big hands under its small arms as he supported its small head with his fingers. He glared at it and said, "Breathe, little one! Breathe!" No wonder he could not see the baby's face plainly! It was not his eyes not focusing. The baby's head and face were covered with a caul! Gently but quickly, he placed the baby on the mother's stomach and carefully removed the membrane from the head of the baby. He, then, picked up the baby boy, lifted him upward over his head, and looked up at it and demanded, "Breathe!" He squeezed the infant's chest and relaxed his fingers several times. He closed his eyes really tight and repeated his admonition. The infant coughed a weak cough and jerked its arms and legs. Then it took a deep breath and let out a loud wail. Solomon opened his eyes and smiled.

"Ahieee!" shouted the Frenchman.

His wife cried tears of joy. Solomon handed the wiggling baby to its father, who handed it to his wife. The Frenchman grabbed Solomon and danced around, babbling away. "*Merci. Merci beaucoup. Merci.*"

The man twirled Solomon around. Solomon felt dizzy and passed out in the middle of the floor of the house. He felt and sensed nothing.

"*Bon ami*," said the Frenchman, looking at Solomon. Solomon looked up into the man's smiling face. Solomon was lying on a narrow bed on the other side of the little one-room house. His head was bandaged. He heard the baby crying softly on the big bed. "Antoinette! Antoinette!"

The woman came over, stood, and looked at Solomon. "*Docteur? Septieme fils d'un septieme fils?*" she said and gazed at Solomon with thankfulness on her face. She said more words in French quickly and moved to pick up the infant, and returned to show it to Solomon. "*Merci beaucoup. Merci.*" She held the baby at a better angle for Solomon to see. "Louis *Petit* Louis. *Bon.*" Antoinette smiled broadly. She moved so that she could kiss Solomon on the forehead. "*Merci. Merci.*" Events were still blurry and confused to Solomon. But he was feeling better, and all his senses were slowly returning to their normal functions. But he still felt exhausted and somewhat disoriented. He knew he needed more sleep.

"Pierre. Pierre," said the man as he pointed to himself. "Pierre."

His wife came back, and he pointed to her and said, "Antoinette. Antoinette." He grinned and put his arm around her. *"Vous reposez,"* he said to Solomon. Solomon's eyes closed, and he slept.

The French couple took care of Solomon while he recuperated from his accident. He stayed with them for two and half days longer. He understood some words they spoke in their Cajun French, and they knew some English words. He communicated his name and home to them. He learned their last name was Guillot. He told them he was going to Marksville.

Pierre had Midnight ready when Solomon was to go. Pierre pointed the way to Marksville. Solomon mounted Midnight, waved at the couple and the child, and started toward Marksville.

It was a clear day with bright sunshine. Solomon passed several small houses along the trail. He continued. There was a two-story wooden house set back from the road. Soon there were more houses on each side of the road. One house caught his eye as he slowly approached. He slowed his horse Midnight even more. It had a front porch with an old man sitting and smoking on it, watching two small boys and a little girl play on the grounds in front of the house. As Solomon came closer riding Midnight, the girl chased the boys toward the on-coming horse and rider. "Yew chil'ren gits back here! Git out of de way of dat man!" Solomon tipped his hat to the old man and kept riding.

In a few minutes he turned down what was the main street of the little town of Marksville. He passed a post office on his left.

People were going in and out of the building. He could hear many people talking French or Cajun and sometimes English.

The street was dirt with a ditch just in front of the board walkways along the front of the mostly wooden buildings. Wooden walks bridged the ditch ever so often in front of the buildings.

Marksville itself was a cluster of houses and buildings around what was the courthouse. The Marksville courthouse was a two-story brick structure larger than the other buildings around it. There was a tavern nearby. What caught Solomon's eye was a tall wooden gallows standing near the courthouse. To Solomon it cast an ominous shadow. To the people walking about and in and out of the buildings, it was just something there, it seemed, for them to walk around and ignore.

Solomon halted Midnight in front of the tavern, dismounted, tethered him, and went in. He came out an hour later and led Midnight over to a mercantile store and tied him to a post. Solomon went in and came out in a few minutes with supplies. He had been told of the Indian mounds nearby while in the tavern when asking questions about the geography of the area. He would go there to think and perhaps sleep the night under the stars. As boys he and Sawyer had camped out on the Indian mounds near Natchez. He remembered the night they had stayed on top of the Emerald Mound and how he and Sawyer looked at the stars and talked about the future. The Marksville mounds would be a good place to think and to plan his next move. He and Midnight came upon the mounds before he knew it. He tied his horse to a sapling and walked. There were five mounds, none of them nearly as large as Emerald Mound near Natchez. Each was about twice as tall as he was. One of them was somewhat larger in area than the others. Pierre's cabin would fit on top of it quite easily with space to spare. On this mound was a smaller mound of earth, something resembling a raised platform. Solomon stepped up on it and surveyed the area. He saw no one else. The sky was still clear. The night would be clear, too. He would sleep here tonight after he watched the night

95

sky for a time and ponder his future considering what Grandma Dundee had told him.

That night Solomon Witcher, atop the largest and highest mound, watched the stars in the clear night sky. The moon rose and gave everything a pale light. He gazed at the heavens and wondered about Eve and Miriam and the Dundees. He wished he knew where he was headed. He remembered Grandma Dundee. He wished he knew what would compel him to stop and begin digging to unearth Murrell's silver. He took the pouch from about his neck and emptied the silver piece onto his palm. He thought about the small metal box, the gift from Grandma Dundee. He thought about the Cajun baby born with the caul. He looked upward and wondered again. The silver coin slipped from his grasp and fell to the ground as he said aloud, "I need to know." He looked away from the sky downward to the grass where the silver piece had fallen. He saw its silver sheen from the moonlight and picked it up and said again, "I need to know."

That night Solomon Witcher slept well. He rose early at daybreak and began his quest once more.

Days passed. Solomon and Midnight had traversed the area many times, it seemed. Solomon was becoming impatient. He went back to Marksville for additional supplies. He rented a bed for a night at the Bell Tavern. Before he slept, he found a friendly poker game to engage himself for a while that night to get his mind off his quest. Some interesting characters participated in the poker game in the back corner of the large tavern room. The most intriguing individual was a young man with the last name of Riddle. Riddle was full of questions about everybody at the poker table. He was a talker. Solomon thought that Riddle must be a lawyer with all his questions. Another player became annoyed by the constant onslaught of questions from Riddle and clammed up, refusing to answer any more questions not directly related to the card game. Riddle kept asking Solomon, "Why are you so lucky?"

Solomon shrugged off most of the luck questions and continued to focus on his cards and the faces of the other players. Solomon could sense a winning streak. He concentrated on his cards to keep winning the rather low-stakes game in this little town. One of the men injected into the conversation the subject of the faith healer that had passed through the area in recent months. Another player asked, "Ya mean dat man dat brought de Guillot new-born baby back to life?" Solomon felt a bit uneasy. He hoped no one knew that he was the person who had helped the Guillot infant. He did not want attention.

"Non, I mean da red-headed woman dat healed old man Tassin in town and dose Chatelains over to de west."

"What happened?" asked Solomon quickly.

"Me? Dats all I know except dey say she was fair-skinned and beautiful."

Another player added, "Dey say she done wore a red string at her ankle. Tink dat was a sign of her power? But dats all I kin say 'bout her, too. Dey say she done left de Mocksville area after bein' here only a few days. She be gone afore we knowed it." Solomon just listened. He won several of the next hands and decided it was time to leave the game. He excused himself from the table and went up to his room to sleep.

The next morning he went to visit the Guillots. Little Louis was well and growing. He could cry out loud now and be heard outside the house. He stayed the night with Pierre and Antoinette and their infant. The next morning he rose and sat on the small front porch with Pierre. He told Pierre, who understood practically nothing of what he said, about his hunt for John Murrell's silver and gold. Pierre smiled and nodded his head ever so often. Solomon decided while talking to Pierre that he would ride along the river bank where possible from here to below Marksville and then back to Alexandria. If he

97

found nothing to indicate where to dig, he would cross the Red River at Alexandria and ride the north side of the river downstream as far as he could.

He exchanged farewells with his French friends and rode toward the Red River. He was optimistic now.

Solomon reached the river. Its water was a rusty red color. He knew easily how it had gotten its name. He turned Midnight to head downstream. It was easy going at first, but then the undergrowth became heavy, and Midnight slowed. The horse plodded on. Solomon still waited for some feeling of an indication. The day was hot. Swear poured down his back. He put his hand on the pouch hanging down from his neck. He pressed his hand against the pouch and his chest.

He rode on for an hour or so. He was anxious again. Midnight stopped near the trunk of a giant oak tree that had fallen not too long ago. It looked to have been struck by lightning. It had probably happened the night of the bad storm, the night that he had fallen, he thought. There were several saplings and other bushes around.

Solomon took advantage of Midnight's stopping to reach for the pouch. He slipped the silver piece out and held it in his sweaty hand. He squeezed it hard and said, "I need to know." He closed his eyes. The silver piece slipped from his hand and dropped to the ground. "What?" he said angrily. "Now where is it?" he added, opening his eyes. He glanced downward, sweeping the ground around Midnight's right flank to see the shiny silver coin. He saw the silver shine from catching a ray of sunlight. It had lodged between the roots of a young tree. "There it is," he said with a happiness in his voice. He dismounted Midnight to pick it up when he realized that the tree was a scraggly sycamine tree within a patch of smaller ones near a larger, fuller one.

"Oh, my God! Grandma Dundee had told me all along. I know this is the spot," he exclaimed. He felt an elation overwhelm his whole body. He tied his horse to the trunk of the fallen tree and just stood there looking at the sycamine. He retrieved the coin and placed it back into the pouch.

The young sycamine tree was indeed scraggly with only a few small branches. He looked at the tree and then at the nearby river. The tree was about as tall as Midnight's back and had few leaves on it. Solomon reached down to grasp the one-inched trunk and gave it a yank. He ripped up roots and dirt. He pulled again and disconnected the tree from the earth. He held it tightly and carried it over to the river, stood on the bank momentarily, and then threw the sycamine into the water. He watched it float away. Now he would dig.

A giant oak tree's main roots and partial trunk was still standing only ten feet away from where he had uprooted the sycamine. He looked and thought about how majestically the great oak must have stood before the lightning had struck. "It must have been the tallest tree, the landmark of the area," he thought. "Something John Murrell might have used to mark his money burial site and to camp under because the tree was massive in size and obviously had been there for generations."

Solomon went over to Midnight and removed the saddlebags. He sat back on the fallen tree trunk and opened one side of the saddlebags. He felt Grandma Dundee's old metal box. He took out a small spade blade that he had purchased for the journey. At the spot where the sycamine had been growing, he dropped to his knees, pulled on two roots that had snapped and remained in the ground, and then, holding the blade in both hands, started the slow process of scooping dirt, enlarging and deepening the hole.

An hour's digging gave Solomon nothing but tired arms and a sore back, but he persisted. He struck a few rocks several times. He kept digging. He stopped to wipe the sweat from his forehead and got up to fetch a drink of water from his canteen still on the saddle. In a few minutes he was digging again. He unearthed some deteriorated pieces of leather and struck something hard. He scooped slowly now. He put the metal utensil aside and used his hands and fingers. It was a bone. He scooped again. Another bone. He dug faster. He hit something again. It was larger. He plunged his fingers down into the earth and pulled upward. Dirt flew everywhere. He reeled back in disgust. He had unearthed a skull, a human skull!

"If this was meant to scare me, it did," said Solomon to his horse. "But it won't scare me away."

He continued digging up more human bones. He changed his direction somewhat and found more rotten pieces of leather. And then a scoop pulled up a dirty silver coin. The next scoop brought three! He reached into the damp earth with his hands and grabbed a double handful of dirt permeated with silver pieces. He examined one. Some type of foreign coin. Maybe Spanish. He kept digging and pulled out the remains of a large leather pouch, which had been filled with silver pieces. He continued his excavation. Now he unearthed United States' coins.

Solomon dug the hole deeper and deeper until it seemed the cache of coins ended. Now he dug the hole wider all around. He found more coins. Next he unearthed a thick leather pouch. Some of the leather had deteriorated and almost had some holes in it, but whatever was inside was probably not harmed by the lengthy burial. Solomon began to untie the leather thong that had been wound around and around the pouch to keep the flap secure against the body of the pouch. It broke in his attempt. He pulled it from the old pouch. He unfolded the flap upward and backward, pulling the enclosed pouch open to reveal a thick wad of currency—United States government currency. A few bills were a little moldy, but the closed pouch had protected the bills remarkably well. He was ecstatic and dug deeper furiously. Then

100

his digging revealed nothing but dirt. He had found foreign coins and United States coins. Most of the coin mix was of silver and gold. He had hundreds of coins—large and small in size. He had too many for his saddlebags to hold! He realized that he would have to re-bury some of his newly acquired treasure. He packed as many in his gear as possible and filled all his pockets to appear as if they held something but did not bulge with the obvious. He knew that he must go back into Marksville to that bank he had passed several days earlier. He knew that he must make at least another trip to the burying site. He would be discreet; he would spend another night or two at the Bell Tavern and then return to his treasure with an additional saddlebag.

Solomon filled in the area where he had dug and selected a spot thirty paces north to rebury the coins he could not transport. He chose several landmark features to help him remember the new burial site of his treasure. He covered the original dug hole and the newly dug one with leaves and fallen branches and sticks to make them seem more natural and somewhat undisturbed by any humans.

As he traveled back to Marksville, he was ecstatic inside but calm on the outside. He focused his attention on his surroundings and any other travelers he encountered. In Marksville he rode past the gallows again, feeling a certain creepiness as he did. He stopped in front of the local bank, took his saddlebags from his horse, and went inside—much to the delight of the bankers there. Arrangement were made for money transfers to Baton Rouge and New Orleans. The bank employees who handled the deposit were asked not to announce the new client or talk about the stranger who walked into the bank to deposit a large sum of money.

Solomon now checked in at Bell Tavern, cleaned up in his room, and rested from the day's activities. He slept for a short time and dreamed of old man Holcumb and Grandma Dundee. He awoke at twilight and went down to find food and then a game of poker at the back table. None of the players from before were there this night.

About an hour into the game, Solomon, remembering the story about the woman healer from the last poker game and wanting to be friendly, injected the red-headed healer into the general conversation. He asked why had she had left so suddenly it seemed. One of the players Eugene, a big burly man with a quick wit, asked, "How yew know 'bout dat redhead healer woman?"

Solomon quickly answered, "I was in a poker game here a bunch of days back, and the talk was of a beautiful redheaded woman who had healing powers. She had visited here for a few days and performed her healing work. What happened to her? It was said she left rather quickly."

Eugene, looked at his cards, and then said, "It was de priest. The church people run her out, forced her to leave dis town. Dey doubted her powers. Said dat it could be de devil's work."

"Did you see her?" asked Solomon.

"Naw. Not me, but I wished I did. My hip and knee give me troubles all de time," replied Eugene. "Too late fer me."

One of the other players named Michot piped up and said, "I saw her over to Mansura. I was riding along de bayou late one night when I come up on a group of persons around a big ole bonfire. Dere was her in among de people. Dey say de sick were healed by the dozens dat night. I passed on by, but I heered 'bout what went on t'ree or two days later."

Solomon was curious even more now. "Tell me what you know."

The men stopped the poker game for a time to follow the conversation.

Michot continued, "My cousins be dere dat night. Dey say she a real healer. Dey believe in dat redheaded woman's abilities. Dey say she done healed Aunt Rose's consumption which be hanging on

102

since the yellow fever epidemic in 1855. I ain't saw dis aunt yet for myself. But dey believe!"

"Did your cousins say anything else?"

"Dey did. Dey say she give de Good Lord de glory. Dey say dat woman don't demand any money or nothin'. She onlyest takes what persons wants to give her. Dey say dat woman healer even gives back some coins if'n people gives her too much. Why, one man done give her one of dose big ole Bowie knifes."

"Someone gave her a Bowie knife? Did she keep it?"

"Yea," said Michot. "And, yea, she kept de knife."

Eugene injected, "Yew know about dose big butcher knifes, don't yew, Witcher? With yew being from up dere on the Mississippi at Natchez. Don't I remember yew sayin' yew from up dere?"

Solomon, trying to make the connection, asked, "Why would I know about . . . . " Then it struck him. "Oh, the Bowie sandbar fight years and years ago. Yes, I heard about what Jim Bowie did to get his reputation as the best knife fighter there is."

"Dat's it, my friend, dat's it," affirmed Eugene. "Dat Bowie knife is some kind of a butcher knife. See!" With those words Eugene reached down to his belt and drew his hand and arm up above his head, and pulled it down quickly, surprising everyone at the table, striking the table top with his own Bowie knife. He removed his hand from the knife hilt, leaving its blade stuck deep in the wooden table. Two of the other players had jerked back from the table. Solomon stood, knocking his chair backward, at the action. Eugene laughed out loud and then grinned from ear to ear. He continued to chuckle at the faces of the other players.

"Witcher, yew be careful if'n yew ever meets up wit dat redhead wit dat Bowie knife likes dis here one, huh?" Eugene laughed loudly once more.

Solomon looked at the Bowie knife at length while Eugene told him and the others about its origin. The blade was about nine inches in length and seemed an inch and a half wide. It had a clip point about a third of the front part of the blade. It had a S-guard with the upper part bent forward and the lower part bent backwards. Its handle seemed the size of the average knife, allowing a comfortable hold by a man's hand.

Eugene told about the knife, "Jim Bowie's brother Rezin had the first big Bowie knife made rat here in Avoyelles Parish by a blacksmith name of Jesse Clifft. Some say dat he built it hisself, but I heared and tink dat de blacksmith done made it fore Rezin Bowie. Others be make after dat furst one. Yew see dat clip part of de front of the top of de blade. Dey say dat it, dat point, be for a quicker and deepest penetration and give de owner de stabbing advantage in de knife fights. So, Mr. Witcher, yew's better not plan to mess wit dat redhead woman wit dat Bowie knife she done got dere in Mansura." Eugene bellowed out another big, long, loud laugh. Then he began to pull the Bowie knife from the wooden table. He had to work it back and forth several times in order to succeed in his task. He put the knife away at his belt once more.

"What is that name—Mansura?" asked Solomon. "Is it French?"

Eugene put in, "Dat be a place over in Egypt."

"Egypt? How was a settlement here named Mansura?"

"Some of Napoleon's soldiers dat been wit him in Egypt come here to settle and tought dis area reminded dem of over dere in Egypt. So dey name it Mansura," continued Eugene. "Dat's wut dey done been sayin' all dis time."

The card game continued for another two hours and then broke up. Solomon stayed another night in Marksville, playing cards again.

The third morning Solomon arose and set out to claim the remainder of his fortune. He journeyed northwest again and located his cache of remaining coins. He dug at this place one last time and recovered the coins left there.

Solomon returned to the Guillots' little cabin one last time. He told them of his discovery, asked them to keep it a secret, and gave Pierre a handful of coins, saying, "This is for the future, especially for Louis." They assisted him in packing his coins so they appeared to be innocent traveler's packs. He bade the Guillots farewell and then traveled back to Marksville, looking at the gallows with consternation as he passed. He rode through Mansura and went on to cross the river at Simmesport. He rode on toward Baton Rouge, dreaming of his future.

Baton Rouge, Louisiana

Solomon stabled his horse Midnight in Baton Rouge. He went to the bank where money had been transferred from Marksville. He bought some new clothes. He then took the steamboat to New Orleans. With him he took two items—a valise and a fair-sized travel trunk that he had acquired in Baton Rouge. In the trunk was a little over $3,000 from the find and one of two single-shot Philadelphia derringers manufactured by Slotter & Co. he had purchased in Baton Rouge. In his wallet in his jacket pocket was several hundred more of the discovered paper money. In his left pants' pocket was a half dozen or so silver coins. In his right vest pocket was the other nickel-silver single-shot derringer.

New Orleans, Louisiana

He knew as the steamboat approached New Orleans this morning that he would have to find his bank to deposit most of his money and find a reputable boarding house in which to stay. His steamboat docked with the usual frenzy of activities by the boat crew and the dock workers. As Solomon walked the gangplank from the steamer to the shore, he saw a great diversity of people from blacks to whites, from Asians to Hispanics, and from bankers to gamblers. He hired a young man to carry his trunk and other bag. He knew as he passed bars and bordellos that he must stay in a respectable section of the city near the financial institutions and other businesses that he wished to conduct transactions with. But he thought there were some interesting locations he passed that warranted a visit or two by him once he got settled in the city. He approached a man dressed in expensive clothes and asked about rooming houses in the heart of the city. The man cheerfully directed him to an area where several reputable boarding houses were located. It took him a brisk walk and twenty minutes to reach the area. As he looked down the street, he saw three signs for boarding houses. He decided to try Angelina Ducote's place. He paid the young man a dollar and dismissed him at the front door. Several rooms were available at the time, and he took a corner room with a view of a busy street intersection. Mrs. Angelina Ducote was the proprietor of the boarding house. She was in her late 50s with gray hair pulled back from her face. She was also the cook of breakfast and supper served at the establishment. He asked Mrs. Ducote where his bank was located in relation to the boarding house, and she informed him that it was in walking distance, just a few minutes away. She gave him the directions. When she left the room, Solomon unbuckled and unlocked his trunk and took his money from the trunk, folded it neatly into several groups of bills, placed those in inside pockets of his outfit, and struck out for the bank. There he added $3,000 to his account and asked how possible future transactions could occur. He also inquired about connections with other banks and transfer of money between them. He now set out to find a gentleman's high-stakes private poker game at Aleix's Coffee House that he had heard about while onboard the riverboat traveling to New Orleans.

On the street he asked a passer-by directions to the intersection of Bourbon and Bienville Streets. He arrived after a slow walk at the location and looked at the corners for the coffee house. He found the building he sought. There was Aleix's Coffee House. It appeared to be a saloon to him. The building he thought must be fifty-something years old and was two-story with a wrought iron railing around a porch that extended over the lower floor, roofing most of the walkway on the two sides of the building that were on the street. He had overheard on the riverboat that this was the rumored place where Andrew Jackson and Jean Lafitte met to discuss the defense of New Orleans against the British near the end of the War of 1812. Solomon went into the establishment to see exactly what it was and what was going on at this particular time of the day. It was a saloon, only with what he thought was a fancy, misleading name. Standing at the bar, he ordered a drink and moved to the end of the bar to look the inside of the place over. The walls were built of dank and musty-smelling brick. The inside had a large dark-colored wooden bar with several large wood columns interspersed, supporting the second floor. Large dark wood beams topped the wood columns. People, mostly men, were coming and going through the entrance door from the street. Solomon decided to sip his drink and watch the patrons and the bartender. He listened to whatever dialogue that he could, especially whenever the bartender spoke.

After sipping very slowly two drinks and deflecting several questions from the bartender, Solomon observed that a man with gray hair and expensive-looking clothes went up to the bar and engaged the bartender in conversation.   Solomon overhead parts of the conversation that included the words "poker" and "cards" and "admission ante." He knew he was in the right place. What he must do now would be to talk with the bartender about how to get into the game and when it would begin.

The next time the bartender came over to refill Solomon's drink and ask again if he wanted a green absinthe, which was that establishment's special drink, instead of the drink he was nursing, Solomon enlarged the conversation to say that he had overheard about the poker game tonight. At first the bartender seemed to know nothing about what Solomon had overheard during the conversation between the bartender and the older man. But Solomon became focused and intent on finding out the information he wanted. He felt that inner ability, that inner energy, that allowed him to influence other people kick in as he looked the bartender directly in the eyes. He was determined to get the information and get into that poker game this night.

The bartender named Babineaux mellowed from his previous position of knowing nothing and became rather talkative about the poker game upstairs on the second floor each evening. He informed Solomon that it was indeed a gentlemen's game, but it was a rich gentlemen's gathering and game. The admission ante, which included drinks, food, and cigars, was $200. He told Solomon that the nightly gathering began at 9 each evening and usually went past midnight. He said that the admission ante was to keep out the riffraff and then laughed smugly. He added that he could never play in that game or even get into the room on the second floor. Solomon told Babineaux that he had the admission ante and more and really wanted to get into the game this very night. Babineaux smiled at Solomon and said, "My friend, I am sorry to tell you that it is nigh impossible for you, a stranger to get into the game. I know of only two other strangers to do so, and they did not get in the first time they wanted."

109

Solomon grinned at Babineaux and replied, "Who do I talk to about getting into the game tonight? Tell me now."

Babineaux told Solomon that the owner of the establishment would be coming in any time now and that he was the one to allow people to the gathering and game.

Within fifteen minutes the owner strolled leisurely in, greeting Babincaux loudly. Babineaux immediately motioned him over to the bar, said a few words to him, and looked over at Solomon at the end of the bar. The owner walked over to the end of the bar and then sat at the nearest table, inviting Solomon to sit with him.

"I am Tekel. Babineaux informed me that yew have heard of our gathering and wish to partake in the gaming. He said that yew would not take 'no' as an answer and insisted on speaking with me. Now what makes yew think yew kin git into our gathering? We have reasons to limit our participants to persons we know and kin trust to be civil at all times, especially when they lose their money. I will afford yew the opportunity to talk with me about the gathering since yew already know about it," spoke the man.

"I am Solomon Witcher out of Natchez, Mississippi," said Solomon. "I am in New Orleans to seek my fortune, so to say."

"So yew are seeking a fortune? Yew do not have money now?"

"Oh, I have ample cash to play in your card game several times over I will bet," replied Solomon to the man's questions. "I just enjoy the game and want to raise more funds for future investments I have in mind.

"How can yew be so sure yew will win here at this establishment? We have people who take the poker game very seriously."

"I seemingly was born lucky."

110

"Luck will take yew only so far," said the owner.

"It has gotten me thus far, my friend."

"But yew forgot that yew must first be invited to play and put up the admission ante."

"No, I have not forgotten." Solomon now looked the man straight in his eyes. Tekel did not say anything for a few seconds. He began to perspire on his forehead. His face reddened. Solomon continued to stare at him. The owner began to fidget in the chair and cleared his throat as if he needed to do so in order to speak. Solomon focused even more.

Finally, the owner asked, "Do you have the $200 on you for the admission ante?"

"Of course," came the reply from Solomon as he reached into his pocket for the cash.

The owner took the money, stood, and said to the bartender. "Mr. Witcher will be joining us tonight for the gathering. I had an opening at the table and filling it will make the poker game more interesting for all."

Solomon now stood and shook hands with the owner, saying, "Thank you. I will arrive at nine or a bit thereafter."

"Will yew be bringing an escort?" inquired the owner.

"No."

Solomon now went back to the boarding house to prepare for the evening's activities. He rested as he lay on the bed, thinking about the poker hands he would be dealt, about the reading of other players' faces during the game, and about the mental focus he would need while playing each hand of cards. He washed his hands and ambled down the hall and the stairs to the dining room where Mrs. Ducote was just setting out the evening meal for her boarders. He engaged in the general conversation of the boarders at the meal. He did not mention the poker game he was to participate in this night.

Just before Solomon was to leave the boarding house to walk to the coffee house on Bourbon and Bienville, he checked his money and then located the second derringer and placed it in his pants' pocket. Tonight he knew he was going to win a lot of money. The two small guns would be his protection on the way back to the boarding house in the early hours of the morning. He set off for his destination.

Exactly at nine o'clock Solomon walked into the coffee house. He paused a moment at the entrance, observing all the people there, drinking and laughing. He noticed several very pretty young women, moving about the large bar room area. An old black man loudly played an old piano in the corner. Solomon then went over to the bar to talk with Babineaux who was still there.

Babineaux saw him and said, "I will have someone take yew up to the gathering in a short time. Please wait here."

Babineaux moved behind the long bar a bit and called a name. He motioned toward Solomon. One of those pretty young women came directly to Solomon. "Hello, darling, what kin I do for y'all?"

"Stop your flirtin' with the man, Sisera, and take him up to the gathering on the second floor. He's cut hisself into that poker game up there. Go now, woman," ordered the bartender. To Solomon he added, "Do not be surprised if yew lose most hands and most of your money tonight."

The pretty young woman grabbed Solomon's hand and arm and marshaled him to the stairs to the second floor. She chattered about cards and food and drink all the way up the stairs and along a balcony on the second floor to a doorway at the end. Solomon barely listened to her talk and chose to observe the layout of the second floor

112

and the large bar room from above. They had passed several closed doors on the way to the double doorway of the poker room. Outside that room entrance stood a large white man dressed nicely but with a not-nice grimace on his face. When they approached near him, he seemed to Solomon to look even fiercer with a heavy scowl occupying his entire countenance.

The young woman smiled at the large man and sweetly said, "Hello, Ramley. Yew on duty tonight, honey child?" The man shook his head in agreement. His lack of speech made him seem more ominous. Ramley opened the twin doors wide for the two to enter the poker room. "Here is where I leave yew, Mister. Good luck to yew!" With those words Sisera turned and walked back through the doorway."

Solomon Witcher stood in an open area with a large round poker table at the other end of the room. Seated at the table were eight men dressed in expensive clothes already playing a hand of poker. Six of the eight smoked large cigars, and all the men had a glass of some sort of alcoholic beverage at their places at the table. Behind the oldest man stood a young woman with her hand on his shoulder. She would whisper something in his ear ever so often. Four other youngish women sat talking at a side table filled with food and drink. They stared at Solomon as he stood there. An impeccably dressed, middle-aged black man seemingly appeared from nowhere and asked in a British accent, "Mr. Witcher?"

"Yes," answered Solomon.

"I am Bartholomew. I will introduce you to the other participants in tonight's gathering when they finish playing this hand of cards. Let us observe for a few moments if you please." That is exactly what Solomon wished to do at the moment. He looked around the table at each of the card players and tried to read the character of each in the brief seconds he stared at them. He noted the one that was

113

doing the most talking while playing and the one that lifted his glass of beverage the most during the hand. One sitting in the chair by the empty chair that he assumed was his place at the table heavily puffed on his cigar and did little talking. On the other side of the empty chair was what seemed to be the youngest man there, including Solomon. He noticed that this man had the largest pile of poker chips and a stack of bills. One of the players looked up at Solomon, grinned, and said, "Welcome."

Solomon nodded his head in response but said nothing because the hand was coming down to the show of cards to determine the winner. The youngest man placed his cards on the table and said, "Straight flush, gentlemen. Does anyone beat that?" All the others still in the hand threw their cards on the table and just shook their heads in disbelief.

The man directly across from where Solomon would be sitting said, "Ahiee, yew be the luckiest man! Is yer winnin' streak still runnin' dis night like it did las' night?"

But before the young man could answer, Bartholomew introduced Solomon as the newest player in the gathering. "Gentlemen, here is Mr. Solomon Witcher, out of Natchez, Mississippi. He is here to win some of your money." Solomon began to go around the table, shaking hands and listening to the names of the other players as Bartholomew said them. He started with the man who puffed heavily on his cigar. "Mr. James Barilleaux, Mr. David Prejean, Mr. Jerome Amedee, Mr. Alphonse Jagneaux, Mr. Pierre Chiasson, Mr. Michael Purvis, Mr. Gaston Dubroc, and Mr. Obadiah Roehl."

"Jist call me Obie. We don't much stand on formalities once yew sit at the table and join in," said Obadiah.

The other men agreed and welcomed Solomon to the gathering and the game. "Maybe yew will hep change the luck at dis table," added the individual with the most pronounced Cajun accent. Solomon placed his money on the table. Now quickly and efficiently Bartholomew exchanged Solomon's money for poker chips. He had put down $500 to start his game.

Now the other players told Solomon their names. They were to be addressed as Jim, Dave, Jerome, Alphonse, Pierre, Michael, and Gaston. Solomon sat at the table in the unoccupied chair between Obie and Jerome. He placed his chips on the table as Bartholomew explained the house rules of the game. Bartholomew added one last statement, "No credit, absolutely none!"

Alphonse was the next person to deal. Solomon watched him deftly handle the cards and then looked around the table at the faces of the players. He already knew the lucky one was Obie. But Solomon had a plan. He would not win but a few hands for an hour or so. He would observe and evaluate all the players for a time and seem to be unlucky himself; then he would really concentrate on the game and win.

Obie was indeed the lucky one in the early hands that night. He seemed to win almost every other hand. Solomon was out about $200 when the men agreed to take a break and enjoy the food and additional drink served by the women in the room. Ten green absinthe drink glasses with the absinthe slotted spoons on the rims were lined up on a table. Jim Barilleaux was the first to pick a glass and down it with one or two large gulps. He reached for another and then began to mingle with the women and other players. All engaged in conversation while eating. Solomon noted that the woman who had been at the table standing behind Jerome circulated about the room more so than did the other women. At one point Sisera came back into the room and spoke to several of the men and women on her way to grasp Solomon's arm. She smiled up at him, took a deep breath which exposed her ample bosom even more, and went up on her toes to say, "Remember, darling, that I am heah to make yew feel welcome. Is there anythin' I kin do for y'all? I'll be heah all night."

At that time Bartholomew spoke loudly for all to hear, "We shall assemble back at the gaming table to resume our card game." The men made their way back to their respective seats, and Solomon picked up the cards to deal this time. All the women left the room.

Gaston in his Cajun accent spoke next, "Aihee, my *bon ami*, it is my time to be de lucky one, no?" He did win this particular hand, but his streak ended there. Now Solomon felt his luck or whatever it was kick in as he began to concentrate on the card game. He now had the feeling that the cards were now in his control as would be the other participants around the table. The rest of the night was his. Obie only won an occasional hand, and that was when Solomon did not concentrate on the particular hand. The night ended after two o'clock. Solomon knew that he was a winner, but he did not count his money at the time. He merely stuffed the bills he had traded for the chips he possessed into his various pockets.

The men exchanged "good-byes" and "good-nights" as they filed from the room. Solomon noticed that Jim Barilleaux had a beautiful walking cane he picked up at the door as he left the poker room. Solomon was the last to leave. On the way out he noticed that each player tipped Bartholomew, so Solomon did as well. But he lingered a bit to inquire of Bartholomew about how to get into the gathering and game for the next evening. Bartholomew informed him that he was to pay his admission ante to Babineaux at the bar in the afternoon.

As Solomon went through the double doors, he saw Ramley still standing there. Solomon reached into his vest pocket, pulled out a couple of bills, and handed them to Ramley. "Thank you, Mr. Witcher," he said as the grimace on his face changed into a broad grin. "When will we see you again?"

"At the next gathering."

"Very good, sir," replied Ramley.

Solomon was cautious on the way back to the boarding house because he had heard others talk of the dangers of being out on the streets late at night. While walking briskly to the boarding house, he patted the derringers in his pockets and was observant of his surroundings. He thought that he might buy a small dagger for added protection. One of the other boarders had shown the roomers one evening the cane he had that concealed a rather large knife. He also thought about some of the people he had met at the coffee house. Ramley was an interesting individual, especially when Solomon saw him soften his countenance as he spoke with Sisera. Sisera was pretty, very pretty—and she was friendly, very friendly. He wondered about her background—where she was from and how did she end up at the coffee house. He wondered the same things about Bartholomew. Obie had this charisma about him, and he had an air of confidence, even to the point of arrogance at times during the game. Gaston seemed to be the typical French Cajun—friendly, garrulous, entertaining, and genuine. The player that struck him as most aloof was Jim Barilleaux. He talked the least—both when he won and when he lost. He responded only when addressed directly, but Solomon noted a certain arrogance in his attitude and tone in the times he did speak. He presented a somewhat mysterious figure there among the other gregarious individuals.

At his room in the boarding house, he counted his money. He was over a thousand dollars ahead of what he had taken to play with and buy into the gathering. Solomon knew that he could raise all the money he needed to invest rather quickly if his luck and good feelings held out. He wanted land and slaves to show his wealth just as the rich folk who lived in and near Natchez had. He would have to discuss with his bankers and some other people as to his venue for becoming wealthy. He thought he would see his bankers to discuss finances the next day and buy a nice dagger at a knife shop for additional protection on his nights out.

The next day he did purchase a small dagger. It was seven inches in length with an ivory handle. His second stop in the afternoon was the bank. Here he had a lengthy discussion about his money and the potential of being a part of the slave trade that would include buying slaves from the Upper South and bringing them down to Texas, Louisiana, and Mississippi to sell to planters and others who desired to own slaves. He had some people to contact in the near future. Now he went back to the coffee house to pay his admission ante to Babineaux. That done, he went back to Mrs. Ducote's boarding house for a time to rest and to enjoy the evening meal with other boarders.

Solomon established a routine for himself—win money at the gathering, deposit his winnings at his bank the next day, and return to the boarding house for rest and the evening meal. Rarely did he break the routine because of little or no winning at the poker gathering. Several times over the next couple of weeks his visits to his bank did not occur. But Solomon trusted his gut feelings about winning and his ability to influence others. Soon Solomon would initiate talks with New Orleans brokers in the slave trade. One evening he told the people at the poker gathering that he would not attend for several days. He was going to see more sights in the city. The only player there from the first time Solomon had played was Gaston Dubroc. Most of those players there on Solomon's first night attended only once or perhaps twice per week. Solomon had been the only player to attend every night for a stretch of time. Ramley, Bartholomew, and Sisera were there almost every time Solomon was. Gaston's parting remarks to Solomon included a bit of advice: "Often times dis city of New Orleans overwhelms individuals. It is quite easy to fall into the hands of de wrong people, join up with de wrong people, and become instruments of de wrong people. Watch oneself, my *bon ami*! When de fun is over, be sure de price yew pay is fitting. Come back soon. I need to win some of my money back frum yew!"

The next day Solomon checked with his bank in the early afternoon, found out that the person he needed to talk with about the possibilities of breaking into the slave trade would be at his bank four days from now, and then decided to walk back to the river boat landing to investigate some of those interesting establishments he had seen on the way into the city. He carried his derringers, his dagger, and somewhere around $500. He was happy and assured himself that he was going to have an excellent time with nothing to worry about.

He heard steamboat whistles in the distance. He noticed the differences of the sounds from the various boats. He saw people streaming from the area of the landing at the far end of the street. Now he looked at the various bars, eateries, and bordellos on each side of the street. They all looked rather seamy and low-class in nature. That did not deter him. He was ready to see some of the underbelly of the city. He and Sawyer had ventured down into the seamy parts of Natchez-Under-the-Hill at home several times before they went off to study up North. This area resembled that on the river at Natchez, but it was much larger in area and had a greater number and variety of people. He wondered to himself what New Orleans had that Natchez did not.

Solomon walked slowly, taking in the sights and sounds and smells of the boat landing area. He saw all kinds of business establishments—bars and bordellos, hotels and boarding houses, eateries and equipment shops, clothiers and bait shops, mercantiles and smoke dens, and even a church front. He heard people speaking in languages he did not understand. He observed the strange dress of foreigners. He smelled food aromas he had not smelled before. Ever so often he drew the attention of someone hawking merchandise in a strange accent or broken English. From some doorways he heard alluring female voices promising entertainment and drink. Most of

119

the women calling him wore little clothing that was revealing in nature. Their smiles were tempting, and their voices were sweet. But Solomon kept walking and looking and waiting for some establishment to garner his attention more than the others surrounding it.

And then out of the corner of his eye as he glanced around, he noticed a small store front with a single sign over a fair-sized window with shelves crammed with bottles, shells, trinkets, rocks, books, and small bags and pouches stuffed with tobacco or scents. The sign proclaimed the shop as THE MUSTARD SEED. Beneath the large yellow letters was the following list of items available at the premises: world curiosities, oddities, trinkets, charms, abnormalities, quizzicals, marvels, wonderments, dream interpretations, and fortunes. Then in script were the following words: "Be not curious in unnecessary matters."

Solomon remembered what Grandma Dundee always said about faith the size of a mustard seed. He knew that this shop would be his initial stop this day. He walked slowly across the street to the store front, grabbed the doorknob, opened the door, and entered. Inside the dimly lit shop Solomon stood at the entrance as his eyes adjusted to the low light.

"What be that ye want heer?" The voice was that of an old woman, but Solomon could not trace the origin of the words as of yet. He heard sounds of a rocking chair. A second or two later he located the source of the words. An old gray woman, chewing on some kind of green plant stem, was sitting in a rocking chair in the dimmest corner of the shop. "Be ye deaf and dumb? What be ye heer fer?

Solomon could see much better now. The old woman reminded him so much of his Grandma Dundee that he was startled at first. He quickly recovered his senses and replied, "Your sign about the name of this place reminded me of conversations with my grandmother when she was still alive and I was much younger. She quoted the Bible and espoused the value of faith the size of a mustard seed. You resemble her."

"Yore grandma showed wisdom and caring. Now what ye be heer fer?"

"I don't rightly know. I was just drawn in by your sign."

"Most wants to know the future. Be ye like most common folk?"

"Allow me to look about . . ."

"If ye wants to know yer fortune, it kin be revealed now—not later. I knew ye would visit today, and ye want to know yer fortune. I kin say it now, not later. Now is the time for yew. Git here and sit on that stool in front of mees and place yer rat hand in me grasp now," announced the old woman with such a sense of urgency that Solomon felt and understood. He moved over to the stool and sat, extending his right hand to her enveloping grasp of bony fingers and callused skin. It was as if Grandma Dundee was holding his hand again and he was a young boy once more. But the old woman went silent for a time. Solomon stared at the old woman during this time. She looked Oriental, but her accent was no such thing. He wondered about her past, her experiences, her background.

She held his hand with her left hand and reached with her right hand over to a small table by her rocking chair and grabbed a wooden cup and then put it up to her lips, "Nothing like cool water to soothe and quench." The faint odor of something rather minty floated into Solomon's nostrils. Now the old woman put the wooden cup down on the table once again and grasped Solomon's right hand with both of her hands and squeezed tightly but gently as an old woman would. She went silent once more.

121

Solomon felt the pressure of the old woman's hands around his right hand. She closed her eyes and opened them, saying, "I be Maxzille, and I will he'p ye forsee. I will he'p ye to divine the future—yers and others. I feel that ye be special and fortunate with some power others can never possess, but ye do not understand much of what ye can be or could do." She paused. Solomon waited anxiously for next words, but she did not utter any for a long time. She merely grasped his right hand more firmly.

Finally she said as if she were in a trance, "Ye be puzzled by what ye are destined and by what ye think ye be. Ye be more than ye seem but less than ye seem. When ye meet O'Suilleabhan, ye will be enlightened but not quenched. When ye meet O'Suilleabhan, ye will be challenged but not fulfilled. When ye meet O'Suilleabhan, ye will be enhanced but not completed." Silence ruled for a moment.

The old woman gripped his right hand even more vigorously and said, "A great conflict will arise—in ye and all around ye. Many will perish, but ye will survive; but ye will not be the same as before the conflict." With that, the old woman yelled out as if in pain and crumpled back in her rocker. She released Solomon's right hand. She had squeezed his hand so firmly that he felt pricking all through it until it receded only to a tingle in his thumb. His thumb tingled and throbbed for a few seconds. It ceased, and he looked back at the old woman. She allowed her head to rest against the high back of the rocking chair and smiled at Solomon. Solomon sat, agog. He did not know what to think or what to say. The old woman continued to smile the rather intriguing smile at him.

"Now pay me," demanded the old woman.

"How much?"

"Not how much—what," answered the old woman.

"No money. What do you want?

"I want the red Irish linen gris-gris bag ye will be given afore ye leave this city."

"What is a gris-gris bag?" replied Solomon slowly and quizzically. "How do you know that I will be given that, that thing, you say?"

"Ye wanted yore fortune. Now swear ye will pay the price I demand!" said the woman emphatically.

"I am willing to pay you money or whatever you wish—if I get that thing, that gris-gris bag. When will I get it?"

"Ye will receive the gris-gris bag afore yew depart New Orleans. It look like this. This be the red Irish linen gris-gris bag ye will get—except'n it will have additional items in it representing less than what they seem and more than what they seem. The gris-gris bag must travel from me, heer, to ye by a route of destiny for the two of us and the hawk-eyed Flynn. Ye deliver the gris-gris bag heer afore ye leave the city, do ye understand? There be consequences if ye be not true to ye word," warned the old woman. She held up the red Irish linen gris-gris bag for Solomon to see. He reached to touch it, but the old woman jerked it back from his grasp.

"I understand and will deliver the gris-gris bag as you appoint," answered Solomon. He shook his head, wondering just how crazy she was and how insane he was for hanging on each word of her predictions. "I will do as you direct."

"Yeah, ye will. Now be gone, young man. Fulfill ye destiny and mines," the old woman said as she motioned him out of her shop. "But one thing more afore ye go. Ye tie this heer red string about ye ankle but keeps it secret." She handed him a piece of bright red string she took from the near table. She watched him with keen interest as he tied it around his right ankle.

Solomon arose, walked to the door, opened it, and strode out onto the busy street. The sun was setting. He must have lost track of the time while in the old woman's shop. He traversed the street, got to the other side, and looked back at THE MUSTARD SEED and its sign. He thought of Grandma Dundee, what the old woman spoke, the tying of the red string, and the gris-gris bag she showed him. Then he dismissed his thoughts and joined the flow of people along the street. He needed a drink.

Solomon walked for time with the stream of the people. At one saloon entrance he turned and went in. Music blared from a piano, and laughter and loud conversations demanded the attention of anyone who entered. He went over to occupy an empty space at the bar, ordered a drink, and turned to look over the establishment and its patrons and employees. He noted several tables where men were playing poker, a roulette wheel and table, and several pretty young women. One of the women seemed to be walking toward him until he noticed that she was intercepted by a worker who pointed to a door in the rear of the bar room. She looked over at Solomon, smiled at him, did a faint wave of her left hand, and proceeded to the doorway she had been directed to.

Solomon now put his attention to the poker tables. He wondered if he would feel lucky tonight and began to think about cards and winning hands. He focused for a minute or two while holding his drink. He closed his eyes for an instant until he heard a female voice saying, "Buy me a drink, mister?"

It was the pretty woman who had smiled and waved at him when he first entered the establishment. She smiled up at him. Solomon motioned to the bartender for a drink for the young lady. "My name is Ameline," she said as she grasped Solomon's arm and guided him to nearby empty table. They sat.

Solomon did not resist her overtures for more alcohol and the promise of a good time in one of the second-floor rooms of the saloon. After thirty minutes Ameline stood, reached for Solomon's hands, and led him toward the stairs. He went willingly into the debauchery of the night in the city.

Three mornings later Solomon awoke in his room at Mrs. Ducote's boarding house with the sun brightly shining on his face. He immediately felt in all of his pockets. They were all empty. Raising himself from the bed, he looked at the table near it. No money there—but his two derringers were placed neatly and squarely in the table's middle. No sign of his dagger either.

But he did possess one thing he had not before his adventure—a hangover. His head now ached like two railroad locomotives had crashed into each other. He sat on the side of his bed and waited for the headache to dissipate a little. It did not. He remained on the side of the bed for several minutes before there was some relief. He tried to remember what had happened since he had been here last. He remembered THE MUSTARD SEED sign and shop and the old woman and her story of a gris-gris bag and what he was supposed to do with it before he left New Orleans. He remembered Ameline and drinks and several other young women. He blanked his mind for a few moments. His headache pounded with force more again. He closed his eyes as he sat on the bedside.

Now he focused his mind and pushed the headache into its recesses. He stood and remained motionless for a short time. Then he walked across the room to check his other possessions he had left there. Everything was there. Nothing had been touched or moved. He turned to look at the derringers. He walked over to the table to pick them up. He could tell both of them had been fired. He did not remember doing that.

Solomon washed and changed clothes. He then went downstairs. On the first floor he noted that it was mid-morning. He heard Mrs. Ducote in an adjoining room and went to talk with her. "Good morning, Mr. Witcher," she said enthusiastically. He returned her greeting and hesitatingly asked her what day it was. "Why, Mr. Witcher, it has been three days since I have conversed with you. Just where have you been, and what have you been doing?" she questioned with a knowing smile on her face. She said that it was Thursday.

Solomon uttered sheepishly, "Thank you, Mrs. Ducote." He was going to leave the room, but Mrs. Ducote asked, "Would you like for me to fix you some breakfast? The kitchen is always open for polite and handsome young men." She smiled another smile at him and said, "Come on in the kitchen." He followed her into the kitchen.

Solomon used the rest of the day to recover from his adventure. He read a newspaper in the social room of the boarding house and relaxed as much as he could. He wondered about his dagger—who had it and where it was. The money no doubt had been spent unwisely or slipped from his pockets unknown to him. But now he knew he had to focus on business starting in the morning at his bank. He would give it his full and complete attention.

The next morning he was in his bank downtown as soon as it opened. He transacted his business in an hour or so and turned to the front entrance of the bank to emerge onto the street. Upon stepping out onto the street from the bank, he took a deep breath. He felt he was about to embark upon a grand adventure in New Orleans, a city different from any other he had ever been in. He heard a deep throaty "caw" from a large black and ashen-gray bird atop the façade of the two-story mercantile across the street. His eyes directed their attention to the bird, a crow. At least he thought it was some kind of crow. He had never seen one with such odd coloring. His gaze drifted back down to the street with its bustling traffic and people moving like lines of ants. Directly down from the crow, a rather mysterious figure

126

caught his eye from across the street. The figure was a young woman in a hurry. When the crow had uttered its cry, she paused and looked up at the top of the building, just as he had done. Then, quickly, she directed her attention back to street-level, where she surveyed the people behind her. It was the way she was dressed on this hot, muggy day and her staccato movements that had initially caught his eye. It was about high noon, and she wore a gray cloak with a black hood. She clutched it rather tightly to her body, and its black hood covered most of her head and face. He heard the crow's cry again but did not look up. Neither did the cloaked woman. He stood on his side of the street and watched her go haltingly through the crowd on the other side. Her hurried gait was punctuated with a pause ever so often, accompanied by a backward glance. She had entered his field of vision slightly to his right. Each time she took a backward glance the hood opening teased him with a few strands of brilliantly copper-colored auburn hair. The cloak's narrow vertical opening yielded glimpses of a scarlet dress. All he could tell about her face was that it was pale. Her small hand that pulled the hood closely around her neck and head exhibited two fairly large rings.

Solomon saw her glance backward again and then upward at the façade where the large bird was. He gazed upward as well. The ominous-sounding crow cawed continuously for a few seconds. The fluttered its wings momentarily remaining perched but suddenly flinched and took flight along the street in the direction the mysterious woman was weaving her way through the people along the crowded street. Solomon focused his sight on the bird—some variation of crow he again surmised. It had black wing, tail, thigh, throat, and head feathers. The remainder of its body feathers was an ashen-gray. Solid black glossy feathers covered its head rather like the red feathers of a full-hooded common woodpecker. He had never seen a crow like this one. What a coincidence he thought for him to see the mysterious woman with the gray cloak and a black hood on the street and that

127

black-hooded crow above on the building façade. Now he heard the crow cawing from down the street. He remembered Grandma Dundee cawing like a crow when she told some of her stories to him and his cousins when they were small and would gather around her old rocking chair. Solomon directed his eyes downward to the woman on the street. She had advanced along the street. He could hardly see her now. On a whim, he hastily decided to follow her.

Solomon made his way across the street, darting between horses, carriages, wagons, and other people. On the other side of the street, he turned to follow that woman. He knew that she glanced behind her often and was rather erratic in her pace on the street, but now she seemed to move more quickly and at a steady pace. Solomon picked up his own pace in order to keep up with the woman. He saw her pause and look in his direction. He was close enough and at the right angle of vision through the crowd of people to see her face at the time the black hood and the entire front of the cloak briefly opened. He observed a mischievous smile form on her pale face framed by her amazing copper-colored hair. The she adroitly turned and hurried onward. With his eyes focused on the mysterious woman as he walked, Solomon was unaware of the black and gray cat from the alley darting in front of him. He realized he had stepped on the cat's left hind leg when the cat screeched, startling him and others around him. He stopped in his tracks. Solomon's eyes followed the cat as it scampered out into the middle of the street and then back to the same side of the street. The cat quickly and carefully picked its way back to the boardwalk about fifty feet in front of Solomon. It became lost in the crowd. It was then that Solomon realized he had lost sight of the mysterious woman he had become interested in. His eyes scanned his side of the street, then the street itself, and then the other side. No mysterious, beautiful woman could he find. He abruptly stopped again after walking a few more yards along the walkway. A couple bumped into him from behind, muttering an apology.

He stood, bewildered. People walked around and past him, impervious to his blunted quest to follow the mysterious woman. All he could think about was that bewitching smile she sent his way in that brief moment he could see her face. He, without looking, took a step forward. He stepped on something. There was a screech like that from a hurt cat. He came back to the reality of the hot, muggy day when he heard a woman's irritated voice, saying, "Mister, watch where yew be goin'!" A woman bumped against him, and he removed his boot from her small left foot. "*Sacre!*" screeched the voice, still with the irritated tone.

"Oh, my apologies, ma'm! I was lost in thought. Not paying attention. So sorry," said Solomon hastily and mechanically. He stared at the woman.

"Be yew through eyeing me?" she said as she used her hand to push herself further away from him. Solomon just stood there, speechless. He could not believe all that had occurred since he stepped out of the bank. "Well, *mon cher*, some witch's cat got yer tongue?"

"Ah, umm, you a Cajun?" he stammered.

"What a smooth talker!" the Cajun woman replied in a condescending yet civil voice as she put a respectable distance between them; she then rolled her eyes, smiled at him, and turned to go her own way once again.

Solomon just stood there, looking at her, thinking, "What came over me?" It seemed that he was beguiled by that mysterious redhead's smile and bewildered by this other woman who had bumped into him after he stepped on her foot. He turned to watch her disappear among the people on the street.

He thought as to what to do next. He straightened his coat and then pulled down his vest to make himself more presentable after his bumping into the woman and stepping on the stray cat. "Something's missing!" he said aloud. His hand went to his vest pocket where he had placed the derringer. It was not there. Instinctively, his hand next went to his coat pocket where he had put his wallet. It was not there. He looked down the street where the Cajun woman had disappeared into the crowd. "That little thief!" he uttered in a low voice. He stood in place as people hurried by him.

"Damn," he said in his normal voice.

"Damn Yankees," declared another deep voice with a Cajun accent.

"What did you say?" asked Solomon as he turned and looked at the stranger.

The man grinned at him and repeated, "Damn Yankees." The man with the grin was dressed in shabby, drab blue pants and a tattered faded blue cotton shirt. His belt was a segment of rope, frayed on the ends that tied at his waist. He looked as if he had not eaten in a while. He pulled at the rope ends nervously but looked Solomon directly in the eyes and now said, "Could you help me with a coin or two?"

Solomon was perplexed and dumbfounded at the moment. He uttered in a rather hesitant voice, "That woman just stole my wallet with my money. She picked my pocket." He pointed in the direction the woman went.

"*Dominus vobiscum!*" uttered the stranger. "A woman absconded with your valuables!" Solomon now looked at the stranger in an unbelieving way upon hearing this utterance. "I can sense you are unsettled, troubled, unsure of yourself. Bless you, my son. Peace be with you. God willing, we shall meet again," said the Cajun man in a rather stoic tone and quickly walked away. The Cajun man slipped into the stream of people as Solomon gathered his senses in the aftermath of all that had happened in the last few minutes. He could not believe the characters he had just interacted with in that little time and the oddity that he was not in control of his usual self. He collected his wits and began the walk back to his boarding house a few blocks away. He put his hands in his pants' pocket, grasped the several coins there, rubbed them together, and pulled them from his pocket. He looked intently at the coins in his hand.

"Why didn't I give that Cajun man a couple of these coins?" He walked, thinking about the recent chain of events. "I could have done that." Solomon soon reached the boarding house and went up to his room to ponder the day's events.

He decided to go down to the dining area at a few minutes to six for the evening meal. He felt better, more like his old self again. He had met most of the other boarders last night at the supper meal. Pleasant conversation had ensued among the group. He hoped there would be more interesting topics of conversation again tonight. As Mrs. Ducote placed the main dishes upon the table, she spoke to each of her guests. When she was close to Solomon, she said to him in rather teasing voice, "Why, Mr. Witcher, how nice to have you with us two nights in a row." She gave him a smile and went back into the kitchen for more food. Tonight's menu included red beans and rice, homemade biscuits, fried chicken, and other vegetables along with an inexpensive wine. Seven other guests sat at the table. On the opposite side of the large table was Robert Rubin, a banker from Detroit; Herman Schmidt, a German businessman; Julius White, a cotton merchant from New York; and Louis Bergeron, a local French teacher. Lawrence House, a slave trader from Virginia, sat next to Solomon. Also, on this side of the table were Thomas Brevard, a firearms salesman from Florida, and James Harbor, a traveling songwriter and singer. The dinner conversation at first centered about the hot weather and the wish for some rain for relief from the heat. Someone asked James Harbor about his travels about the country, shows he had performed in, and any really famous actors he had met. He talked of meeting John Wilkes Booth in a Washington, D. C., show he had been involved with. For a time Julius White extolled the virtues of King Cotton as the economic engine of the nation. At one point Solomon asked Thomas Brevard about replacing the Philadelphia derringer that had been lifted at the encounter on the street with the Cajun woman. The German businessman and the Michigan banker quizzed Lawrence House about the slave trade and expected profits. Solomon listened intently to this part of the dinner conversation. He was thinking in terms of increasing his money fund as quickly as possible. The French teacher pivoted the conversation to the life of slaves and free blacks in New Orleans. Solomon wondered if slave culture and slave life here in New Orleans was vastly different than that in and around Natchez, Mississippi. He asked a couple of questions, and Louis Bergeron mentioned Sunday afternoons at Congo Square in New Orleans. Bergeron commented that the Sunday afternoon gatherings were not nearly the large spectacle that had occurred in the past. New city and state legislation had curtailed the numbers of free blacks and slaves that attended the cultural celebrations every week. If fact, he related that on many Sundays no gathering happened. He reassured Solomon that he had heard on good authority that there would be a celebration this Sunday. He said that it was an experience in itself to see and hear and taste the mix of slave cultures in the city. Solomon expressed an interest in going to Congo Square on Sunday afternoon, and Herman Schmidt indicated he would still be in New Orleans on Sunday and would go with Solomon if he agreed. They agreed to meet at one o'clock at the boarding house and then to walk to Congo Square if weather permitted.

Tomorrow was Saturday, and Solomon had no real plans of business until he went back to the bank on Monday morning to check if everything was in order with his accounts; so, he could proceed with his conversations with Lawrence House about money-making opportunities in the slave trade. Solomon thought the slave trade was the most lucrative avenue to venture onto for his purposes.

Saturday morning after breakfast Solomon decided to put business ideas aside and to explore New Orleans and the area nearby the boarding house. He thought he should see parts of the city in the daytime so that he could navigate himself about in the evening hours on other days. He knew that he would be walking all day to get to know this area of the city. Besides, in the back of his mind, he could not escape thinking about that mysterious redhead he had encountered on the street the other day. Maybe, just maybe, he would spot her in the city again. He walked all day, looking at places and people. He did not catch even a glimpse of any redheaded woman all day. He passed some interesting bars and restaurants that he knew he would frequent later while in the city. Solomon even walked by the coffee house that he had heard about on the steamboat and where he had played cards. In the late afternoon he walked as far as the edge of Congo Square before he decided that he was tired and needed to get back to the boarding house for supper. He was keeping a sober head about him for the promise of conducting business agreements the early part of the next week. He would celebrate later. He did not want to be dazed and confused the way he was on the street a few days ago. He would not be taken advantage of again by anyone. Few boarders were there for the evening meal on this Saturday. Solomon did not talk much, and he went up to his room to consider the upcoming events.

Solomon slept longer than he thought he would on this Sunday morning. He was slow getting around, but he was anxious to meet with Mr. Schmidt to go visit Congo Square today. At one, he promptly went downstairs to meet his new friend. Louis Bergeron was in the parlor and asked if he could go along with the two gentlemen. "Of course," both Herman and Solomon replied at the same time. They knew that Bergeron could add to the local color of the visit. Herman, Louis, and Solomon began their walk to Congo Square.

As they approached the area of Congo Square, the sound of drums floated their way. They continued to walk briskly toward the square. The drums pulsed a louder, stronger beat with a driving rhythm that began to engulf them and everyone else in the immediate area. Louis looked at Solomon and Schmidt, grinned, and said in a somewhat louder than usual voice, "Looks as if there are many people here today to celebrate and have a good time. *Laissez les bons temps rouler!*" The men could hear singing to the driving music.

The music and singing rose in tempo and volume. The men entered Congo Square and marveled at what they beheld. The sounds of the myriad of African and Caribbean musical instruments grabbed their attention as they ambled through what seemed a celebrating marketplace from other lands. They were immersed in a throng of people—all kinds of people attired in all kinds of dress. The first aspect of Congo Square that caught Solomon's eye was the bright colors of the various costumes most of the blacks had adorned their bodies with. Orange was the color with the most beautiful brilliant hues. But there were many other bright colors that arrested the men's attention here and there in the busy crowd of people. Most of the non-slaves wore rather drab clothes compared with the slaves and free blacks there.

Ever so often as they walked, they peered down an avenue of vendors of trinkets, crafts, and foods. Enticing aromas of exotic foods wafted their way into the main area where the music and dancing were. People were whirling about and jumping up and down and yelling and singing. Solomon saw something that reminded him of a little house on the river under the bluff at Natchez. He remembered the whole house covered with chicken claws. He also remembered that Grandma Dundee had warned the children about going into that house or even near it. She had cautioned the children about the

134

mysterious ways of voodoo and forms of black magic. What he saw was several dancers who had attached animal tails all over their outfits. Some costumes were constructed mainly of animal furs and skins. Others, especially some of the women, had decorated their costumes with seasonal flowers and other crafted items that Solomon could not identify.

One black woman danced close to Solomon and whirled about at tremendous speed. One of her adornments flew from her costume and landed at Solomon's feet. "Meester, yew be the special one today. Dis heer gris-gris bag picked yew. It be yore charm now. Yew lucky mon!" As he looked at her, she bent down to pick up a red Irish linen bag and placed it in Solomon's hand. She had grabbed his right hand and forced its palm up as she placed the item in his hand and closed his fingers around it with her other hand. She smiled at him and disappeared into the mass of dancers before he could say anything to her. Solomon was astonished. What the old woman told him at THE MUSTARD SEED had come true. He had placed that remembrance out of his mind for a few days. He just stood there. Suddenly the music stopped there close to the three men. Background music continued from other musicians in the square.

Louis took advantage of the relative quietness and declared to Solomon, "I have always heard that any person given a gris-gris bag in the frenzy of a Congo Square whirling dance . . ." A loud cawing occurred just above the three men. Each looked upward to see a black-hooded crow eyeing them from atop the nearby tent. The crow cawed once more and quickly winged itself away.

Herman Schmidt remarked that he had only seen crows like that one in Europe. Louis Bergeron said that he had never seen one with markings like that. Solomon said, "I saw that one or one like it just a couple of days ago here in the city."

"A coincidence?" questioned Louis.

"An omen?" asked Schmidt. "A sign?"

The music began blasting its driving beat once more. Dancers sprang up and began whirling and gyrating to the pulsating beat. The volume seemed louder and more encompassing. Solomon, who had wanted to ask Louis to finish his sentence concerning the gris-gris bag delivered to him by one of the dancers, now had to wait. He knew they would have to walk a bit away from the musicians to be able to hear one another. He motioned to Louis and Herman to follow him to a place farther away from the nearest musicians. Solomon placed the gris-gris bag in his pocket but held his hand over it for its protection.

They began to walk back to the front of Congo Square. Solomon was very interested in what Louis would say about the gris-gris bag, but suddenly his interest was arrested by something or someone else he spied. There at one of the seller's tents he saw a figure in a gray cloak with a black hood. Red hair streamed out one side of the hood. The woman handed the seller money and put what she had purchased into a cloth bag she had with her. She turned and walked toward the entrance to the square. Solomon loudly and emphatically told the other two men, "Wait for me here. I must follow that woman."

Louis and Herman, bewildered by Solomon's abrupt departure, stopped in their tracks. Solomon continued to follow the mysterious woman. He still had the gris-gris bag in his vest pocket with his hand over it. He weaved his way through the crowd but had to slow and almost stop when a huge mass of people was entering the square. He struggled against the flow of persons to reach the entranceway. He quickly surveyed both directions when he made it to the street. He lost her again. He continued to look for a few seconds but still did not see her. He reluctantly turned to go back into the square to join with his friends from the boarding house.

Louis and Herman waited for Solomon but while observing the dancers and other people drifted a bit away from where Solomon had left them. Solomon passed the vendor where the mysterious redhead had made her purchase. He turned to go back to talk with the seller and saw a cat slip between the tent and the one next to it. He thought about the cat he had accidentally stepped on in the crowd of people on the street the same day he first saw the redheaded figure. As he was looking down at where the cat had vanished between the tents, he heard the market place seller call out, "Hey, *mon cher*, yew need a good luck charm? Yew afreered of some ole witch's cat?"

Solomon looked up and saw the woman who was calling out to him. It was the Cajun woman who had stolen his derringer and his wallet! He kept his head down, hoping the woman would not recognize him as one of her victims and slowly walked over to her and her table of charms and other items.

"Step on over to dis collection," the woman said as she motioned him closer. Apparently she did not recognize Solomon from several days ago. She smiled at him as he approached her table of wares.

Solomon pointed to a doll fashioned like a man and inquired about its cost. The woman looked down at the man-doll and said in a soft voice, "Dis here is special. Dis one here yew like is powerful." She carefully picked it up to show to Solomon. As she held it out to him for his perusal, Solomon grasped her wrists and said in a deep commanding yet soft voice, "I am not interested in the man-doll. I am very interested in you and the redheaded woman you had a transaction with a few minutes ago." He held her wrists very tightly now. She tried to jerk away but could not.

"Do not scream or yell for help. I know you are the one who stole from me just a couple of days ago. You attract attention, and I will tell all about you. Just be silent and listen to me. I will let you

137

go if you give me the information that I am seeking." Solomon used his special voice and demanding tone that he had used in the past to get his way with people—the voice he had used to secure the coin from the old man in Natchez before he left.

The Cajun woman looked at him. "Yew. Yew be the one that stepped on my foot on the street corner. Yew be hurtin' my wrists. Please."

Solomon calmly continued to hold the woman's wrists and said to her once more, "I want information about the redheaded woman who had purchased something here a few minutes ago." He squeezed her wrists and looked directly into her eyes. "Who is the woman?"

"A friend, a close friend," she said weakly. Tears welled up in her eyes and ran down both cheeks. "Please do not harm her."

"Why do you think I will hurt her?" quizzed Solomon. "Perhaps I am enamored of her." He persisted in looking the Cajun woman directly in her eyes, and she seemingly let down all her defenses, relaxing her tension against Solomon's grip.

"Your money be gone, but I still gots de little gun. Yew kin have it back. Let me git it from my bag under the table." Solomon relaxed his grip on the woman's wrists and let go of them.

"What is your name?" asked Solomon.

The woman reached down to grab her bag. "Ann," she replied as she raised up, pointing the derringer at Solomon.

"Now you don't want to attract attention, do you?" He looked deeply into her eyes again. She shivered and lowered the little gun.

"Who yew be? Wat kind of pow'r yew master of? Be yew a voodoo mon? Yew like Egypt?"

Solomon looked at Ann intently. "Who is Egypt? Is that the redheaded woman's name?"

"Yea, hur name be Egypt," said Ann slowly. Then she rapidly fired several questions at Solomon. "Yew ever seed hur before? Yew done saw hur on the street the same day yew stepped on me two times? She dun beguiled and bewitched yew, voodoo mon? Egypt dun catched yer eye, and yew looked straight into hur gray-green eyes? She dun outspelled yew, huh, voodoo mon? And all she dun was to look at yew!"

"What do you mean? What are you talking about? No woman's ever beguiled me, much less bewitched me!" shot back Solomon.

"Oh mon cher! Egypt be no reg'lar woman. Her be special. Her and me laugh at yore pitiful little power! Egypt know voodoo, dat Amish magic, and, uh, sorts of other magicals."

"Where is she?" inquired Solomon, in spite of the menacing words from Ann. Ann was silent for a few seconds. Solomon became impatient and set his mind on finding the one called Egypt. He focused his attention on Ann and with a charmed voice said firmly to her as he looked directly into her eyes, "You are going to tell me how to find her." He felt his unique mind strength welling up and focusing on Ann. "And you will not lie to me!"

Ann stared into his eyes blankly. Then she said rather mechanically, "I not lie to yew."

Solomon quickly went between the tents and into the one occupied by Ann and her voodoo items. "Pick up your items and close your tent for now."

"I be doin' dat rat now," Ann said weakly and then proceeded to gather charms, dolls, gris-gris bags, and the other bangles. She pulled the front cover of the tent down, tied it, and turned to Solomon.

"Egypt say her be at the mud flats across de riber tonight at midnight to jern in de voodoo workins. Does yew wants me to take yew dere tonight?"

"Yes, I do," uttered Solomon rather hastily.

"Kin yew gets to de ferry boat dat crosses de riber on the hour?"

"Yes. I saw it yesterday when I was walking about."

Loud voices just outside the front of the tent diverted Solomon's attention from the Cajun woman. From the angry words it seemed a fight was about to break out between two or three men.

"Be dere at eleven!"

Solomon turned toward Ann just quick enough to see her bag of gathered items disappear through the flap at the tent's side. At the same instance one of the men outside had been pushed into the front of the tent. The make-shift display table blocked the man's fall. He quickly recovered himself, got upright, and stepped into the fight that had been brewing for a few minutes. Solomon froze, unable to make a quick decision. He regained his wits and hurried outside the tent to look for Ann. The crowd had increased in size, and the Cajun woman was nowhere in sight.

"Now all I can do is show up at the ferry landing at eleven and hope that Ann shows as well," thought Solomon. He began looking for his friends that had accompanied him to Congo Square. He walked about for a few minutes and then saw Louis and Herman near where they had parted.

As he walked toward his friends, he heard over the music the loud throaty cawing of a crow flying rather low over the area he was walking in. The cawing tapered out and died into the music of the Congo Square. He wondered if the crow's cawing was some kind of sign. He wished he could talk for a few minutes with his late Grandma

140

Dundee to hear her interpretation of his continuing some type of relationship to that crow and what it meant. He moved quickly to his friends who greeted him with smiles and questions about his time away from them. He avoided answering their questions by posing one of his own to Louis, "What were you starting to say about someone being given a gris-gris bag by one of those whirling dervishes in Congo Square?"

Louis replied, "Let's talk about that as we walk back to the boarding house. The music is loud here. Is that all right, gentlemen?" The other two men nodded in agreement, and the three turned to exit Congo Square.

"Here is what I have always heard about the gift of the gris-gris bag," began Louis as they slowly walked, distancing themselves from the loud music and the crowd. "First of all, it is not a curse, although I have heard rumors of bad things happening to some of the alleged recipients of the magic bags. The so-called normal gris-gris bag is used to push away evil or to bring about some sort of good luck. The kind of gris-gris bag it is determines what is placed in it and what happens at the ritual that empowers it. It is said that the most famous voodoo queen of the city is Marie Laveau. Her personal gris-gris is said to have contained stones, bone bits, goofer dust from graves, and other things known only to her. The gris-gris bag is some sort of magical talisman to protect and enhance the owner and his powers. Now your gift of the gris-gris bag here in Congo Square is meaningful in others ways. Not all the ways are known to the general folk. Supposedly, the person to whom the bag is presented is said to possess some kind of rarity that most people do not have. Nothing I have ever heard actually pinpoints or defines that rarity. It could be good or evil—like the gris-gris bag itself. It is an omen of something unusual or momentous that will soon occur. It often is a change of fortune or a meeting of an influential person in the individual's life or even a sign of calamity."

"What are you saying to me? Should I be concerned for my safety and the safety of those about me?" asked Solomon. He took the gris-gris bag from his pocket, and they all looked at it.

"No, not necessarily," replied Louis. "Let me tell you all that I have heard associated with this gift."

"Please go ahead. This topic is of great interest and intrigues even me," added Herman. "I know that Solomon wants to know everything about it."

Louis continued. "Whatever is the consequence or signal of the gris-gris bag occurs within a few hours or a few days of the awarding of the gift bag. Something always is a result—good or bad. Rumor holds that the good or bad ultimately depends on the individual and his rarity—the same little gris-gris bag has different effects on different individuals. One's inner self controls the rarity or ability, and that core control with its inherent good or evil dictates the immediate effects and the long-term consequences or results. The charm or spell or whatever it is has a continuous and cumulative effect for the individual presented the gris-gris bag. Even one's fate can be altered in the long run." He paused and then continued, "Oh, one other observation. The bag you have appears to be red cloth. Most gris-gris bags I have seen or heard about have not been that particular shade of red. It may or may not possess additional meaning."

Herman interjected in a laughing voice, "We will have to be cautious on the walk to the boarding house, my friends!" He laughed out loud.

Louis laughed a bit as well, but Solomon took the remarks more seriously than his friends. He had not told his friends about the old woman at THE MUSTARD SEED and what she had told him. He just smiled and thought about his meeting tonight with the Cajun woman and a possible encounter with the redheaded woman called Egypt on the other side of the river. He had much to ponder.

The conversation turned to other topics. The men continued their walk back to the boarding house. Solomon reached into his pocket and clutched the gris-gris bag. He wondered about what rarity he might possess and what would happen. He added some words to the walking conversation but not much. The men reached their destination, and all indicated that they would be eating the evening meal when served at the regular time. They parted, going up to their individual rooms. Solomon's thoughts turned completely to what Louis had said about the gris-gris bag. He wanted to treat it lightly, but he knew that Grandma Dundee had often told him that he was special and had a special gift that he should recognize and use. He could see her face in front of him and thought he felt her hand and then her embrace. He could also see the old woman's face from THE MUSTARD SEED shop. He could not treat anything lightly now.

The loud knocking at his door awakened him from his slumber-like trance. He had fallen asleep in the chair after he had sat and propped his feet up on the bed. He was still clutching the red gris-gris bag he had been given in the square. "It's almost time to eat. Are you going down as you said?" It was Louis at the door.

"Just a minute, my friend," yelled out Solomon. "Wait there for me." Solomon ran his fingers backward through his hair, got up, and went to open the door.

Solomon and Louis walked down to the dining room together. Louis said that he particularly liked the banjo music of one of the groups of musicians at the square.

At the evening meal Louis and Herman told the other boarders of an interesting man they had encountered at Congo Square when they were separated from Solomon. The man had a distinct Cajun accent and wore shabby-looking, drab blue pants and an old tattered faded blue cotton shirt. His belt was a piece of rope, frayed at the ends and tied at the waist. He looked thinner than he should be and had a

143

hungry look about him. They said the man with the obvious Cajun accent spoke articulately with them. They had come face-to-face with him as they made their way through the throng in the square. He was standing in front of a group of dancers, observing them and spouting Shakespeare. He was saying, ". . . romance is like a dance: it has its own rhythm and timing. Look, the three stages of romance are like three different dances. The wooing is like a Scottish jig: hot and fast and full of whimsy and illusion. The wedding is like a dance you would do before the king: proper and decorous. Finally, you get to the part where you regret having gotten married in the first place. It is like the lively cinquepace: it goes faster and faster until you eventually topple over and die." He was facing the front line of the dancers and musicians and turned sharply to face the men in mid-pronouncement. He broke from his quoting, became silent for an instant, and then smiled at them, asking them for a "coin or two."

"The man looked just like a priest or monk of some religious order—just without the robes. He had a certain look about him and the way he spoke, the quoting of Shakespeare, his deep voice with a marked Cajun accent, his demeanor," explained Louis.

"Yes," added Herman. "His way with words. The way he looked at us when both of us handed him several coins. It was genuine gratitude."

Louis continued about the man, "His manner of thanking us, too. He smiled a gracious smile and looked intently at us and said, 'Peace be with you, brothers. God willing, we shall meet again.'"

Herman, after a pause, said, "Yes, he made an impression on the both of us. He seemed so simple and so Godly. He must have been down on his luck for a time. I know he was hungry; he looked too thin for his body frame. I am glad that we gave him some money. He was unlike any other hungry beggar I have ever seen."

144

"Yes, I really hope to meet that Cajun man again one day," said Louis. "I conjecture that he has many stories to tell that would hold my interest. Perchance a future encounter will occur."

Solomon kept silent about his encounter with the Cajun man until now. "I saw the man you two are talking about on the street near the bank the other day. He asked me for money the way he did the two of you. But it was immediately after someone had picked my pocket of my wallet and derringer. I did not give him any coins, even though I had several in my pocket. I was still reeling from the realization of the pick pocket. I regret that I did not give the poor man something!"

"If I see that man again, I will purchase him a meal and talk with him," put in Louis.

The conversation turned to other subjects for the remainder of the meal. The food was delicious, and thus the conversation was reduced. Other boarders began leaving the table for events in the evening or just going up to their rooms. Solomon, when asked what plans he had for the evening, told the others that he was tired after the day's events and would seek respite from the city for the night. He thought he should not tell the others of his possible midnight rendezvous with the redheaded mystery woman. But about an hour before he was to leave the boarding house, he decided to leave a note on the table by his bed. The note to Louis said that he was going to the mud flats on the other side of the river for a midnight voodoo experience. When he completed writing the brief note, he folded it and placed it squarely on the night table by his bed. He knew the boarding house owner would deliver it to Louis if he were not back early enough to destroy the note. He was not really afraid of anyone whom he might meet, even though he knew that other side of the river was even more lawless than the city proper, but he was very apprehensive about the possibilities of the voodoo in light of the gris-gris bag he had been presented.

145

Solomon exited his room quietly and went downstairs to the street entrance of the boarding house. He closed the door behind him and stepped out to the street quickly to go meet the ferry in order to cross the river. He placed his hand in his right coat pocket and clasped the gris-gris bag, wondering what was in it and what was in his immediate future. He picked up his pace and disappeared into the darkness of the streets. As he approached the ferry landing, he could hear the ferry coming in to this side. He saw the lights of the landing and could discern several figures moving closer to the gangway area in order to board the incoming boat. He heard dogs barking, people shouting, and a single cat screeching. He walked faster to be sure to make the boat landing and its departure on the hour. He could now see that the main body of would-be ferry passengers had separated from one petite figure. That figure turned to look his way, and he recognized Ann. She was there. He had worried that she would not show, but she was there, waiting for him to arrive. She must have known that he was Solomon because she walked a bit toward him. As they moved closer together, she said, "Yew slow, voodoo mon. I be here for a time waitin' fer yew. Me be 'bout to leave dis place. I onlyest stay here cuz yew has dat charm 'bout yew dat I be swayed by. An' I be wantin' my mistress to cast her eye on yew."

"Your mistress? Egypt? Are the two of you in cahoots in this magical voodoo mumbo-jumbo?"

"Mistress Egypt save me. I be hur servant because I owes hur, but she say nots really. She rescue me some time ago up in Avoyelle Parish neer de town of Mocksville. Her be trav'lin' tru up dere on her'n way to Nawlins. She done tole me dat I be free to do and go as I pleases. But me, *mon cher*, I stay close to Mistress Egypt. I hep hur wid dat she want me to," related Ann.

"She has money for both of your needs?"

"Yes, sur, Egypt gots money when she want to hab money."

146

"What do you mean by that? Is she wealthy?"

"Me, I don know any more dan dat. I jist be grateful for Mistress Egypt. I not axe hur nuthin'."

"How did the two of you meet?"

The ferry crewmen called for passengers, and Solomon paid for both. The two walked onto the ferry and continued their conversation as the boat readied to leave this bank of the Mississippi River for the other side. The ferry made its way into the dark, muddy water to get to the other landing. Ann and Solomon went to one side to lean on a railing and talk.

"Yew be bery curious, ain't yew, Mr. Voodoo Mon?"

"Yes, I am. And you will tell me what I want to know," added Solomon in a focused voice while looking Ann directly in the eyes. "So tell me how the two of you met now."

"I be tellin' yew now. Up dere in Avoyelle me be walkin' to de little cemetery out in de wood where me little baby be buried. When I cud slip away after chores in de evenin', I go visit me little baby."

"What happened to your baby?" inquired Solomon.

"He catched the cough and de crud, and nobody cud hep him. None of dem healers or dat doctor my old mistress Eleanor called. Me little baby died in dees arms of mine. I puts my hand on his little forehead and felt the fever rage. His little body was hot as fire, and he coughed and coughed. One minute he be at rest and at peace. He grinned up at me, gurgled some noise, and den done took a last breath." Ann was crying and turned away from Solomon to look at the lights on the other bank.

"I am sorry," put in Solomon.

147

Anne turned back to look up into Solomon's face. "I tink yew know my pain in some way. I tink yew even remove some of it from me. Yew got some kind of magical 'bout yew." Solomon gave her a warm smile.

"But here be how me met Mistress Egypt. I be walking to dat cemetery at twilight. I walk on dat dirt road and be almost dere when I feel me a creepy feeling crawlin' all up and down my backbone. I see de cemetery wid its broken down wooden fence around it. But yew see, me little baby not be buried inside de fence. He cain't be in dere wid dem folks withouts no permission. I secretly buried me little baby jist outside de fence at one of de corners of dat cemetery. Me pore little baby."

"Yes, yes. Go on."

"Well, me gots dis creepy feelin' like I done tole yew. I becomes scared, real scared, scarieder dan I ever be. As I walked, I turned dis head o' mines to peek into de thin woods alongside of dis dirt road. I seed dis figure, dis person, dis ting a walkin' along side of me jist a few steps partin' us. Me cud not tell if'n it be a man or a woman or an angel or a devil. Den dis cold chill gripped ahold of my body. I shook. Buts I kept on a walkin' towards me little baby grave. De figure done de same as me. I stop in my track. It stop in its track in dat wood. Den me taught I not look at de figure. It be gettin' dark 'bout den. I mades my feet to walk on. Den as I came up de road, I gots de scares agin and decided to sits at de roots of a big old tree. I done it. I closed both of my eyes to see if'n me cud hides from dat, dat, whatever it be."

"You tried to hide at the base of a big tree?"

"Me done it, too. When I opened my eyes agin and peeked into the edge of the wood where it had been, it be gone."

"What? What happened next?" asked Solomon.

"I be reliefed and closed my eyes agin. I prayed to Jesus dat I be alls by myself jist to visit me little baby in his final resting place. Den me felt that creepy feelin' agin, and I opened my eyes. Dere, rat dere in front of me is dis beautiful woman in a gray cloak with a black hood. She be smilin' at me from dat beautiful face wit dat red hair streaming down along de sides of dat face. Rights behind her de full moon appear. Its light make her look likes an angel from Jesus. I must have passed out rat cold rat den. I remember dreaming dat I could write and was writin' in some kind of book while a woman's cheerly voice be tellin' me what to write."

"What were you writing?"

"Me? I dunno what dat writing be. I not read or write— excep'n now dat de Mistress taught me a little readin' and writin'. But I dose not 'member all dat writin' in dat dream."

"Well, what happened next?"

"When I's come to, all my eyes could see was dat big moon up higher in de night sky. I looked aroun' for dat redheaded woman but did not see her dere. I talked to myself and said, "Sweet Jesus, she be gone!""

"No, I am still here," said a voice from the other side of the big tree I be leanin' on.

"Whose voice was it?"

"It be Egypt. Dat woman's voice be so pretty, so charmin'— except'n when I be so sacred at time and when she rile up and become so mad!"

"What do you mean?"

Ann stopped the conversation when the ferry boat crew shouted and started preparing for the landing. Solomon and Ann remained silent until they disembarked. Ann led the way off the ferry

149

and said, "Dis way!" She pointed into the dimly lit distant area beyond the saloons and brothels and shops and then hurried through the lighted area into the darkness with Solomon right behind her. She was not talkative for a long time.

Solomon wondered to himself how much longer it would take them to get to their destination and how he would react to another encounter with the mysterious redheaded woman. He followed closely behind Ann until she abruptly turned and stopped, almost causing him to bump into her. Ann in a crisp voice said to Solomon, "Wait here fer me."

Ann practically disappeared like magic. Solomon stared into the direction she had gone. There were some scrubby-looking trees, some swamp grass, and areas of unsure footing they had come through. Up above was the night sky blanketed with thousands of stars and the moon that was just rising. He had waited long enough for the moon to rise higher and begin reflecting light to illuminate the night much better than when Ann had departed. No clouds in the night sky allowed the full moon to achieve its full glory of lighting the night. Now Solomon began to hear nighttime noises of the swampy mud flats—frogs croaking, dogs barking, cats screeching, and some other awful sounds he had never imagined. "I hope there are no hungry alligators out here with me," he spoke aloud.

"Alimagators, *mon cher*, dey be *beau coup* of dem crawly creatures all out dere in de night," said Ann's voice from the darkness to his left. She then appeared as if by magic.

"Where have you been?"

Solomon heard a distinct fluttering of feathers and a cawing sound from the darkness to his left.

But before he could say anything to Ann about the noise, she answered his question, "I been seeking out Zethro." She paused.

"An' he be rat heer."

With those words a massive black man stepped into Solomon's view from his left side. Solomon reached for his derringer in his pocket, but Ann noticed and quickly said, "No needs to fear Zethro. He another follower of Mistress Egypt."

Zethro's deep bass voice sounded eerie here in this outdoor setting with the full moon's light. "Naw, sur, no needs to be afeered of Zethro if'n yew be a true friend of Mistress Egypt." But Solomon had doubts about fearing Zethro. Zethro was every bit of six feet six inches tall, a large brawny black man in his late twenties weighing over three hundred pounds. He was muscular with huge biceps on big arms almost as big as Solomon's legs. Zethro's clothes were typical slave clothes that were patched and otherwise mended and drab in color. He tied his overly large pants with a long piece of old rope and had one suspender on the left side of his body that ran up to and over his left shoulder. His gray shirt had its sleeves ripped out at the armpits, and it accentuated his huge biceps. But for some reason, even out here in the rather dark swampy mud flats across the Mississippi River where lawlessness and voodoo were prevalent, Solomon took comfort in Zethro's words about not having to fear the big man. Now Solomon noticed something on the suspender arm that went up Zethro's body. There was some kind of pin or charm attached to it. Solomon could not make out exactly what it was. But what Solomon could distinguish in some sort of belt scabbard at Zethro's waist was a large knife, the Bowie knife he heard talk of in Marksville. Solomon's usual confidence in himself began swelling in his psyche, and now he was ready to face whatever encounter that would occur this night. He now took a long look at Zethro's rather boyish face as Zethro said in his deep, slow voice, "Miss Ann say dat yew possesses some magicals like Mistress Egypt. Yew hep de Mistress?"

"I do not really know your Mistress Egypt. I have only seen her twice. I intend to meet her. I will help her if I can. But right now,

151

she is a rather mysterious figure to me. There is much I do not understand. I need to meet her face-to-face tonight," uttered Solomon.

"I takes Miss Ann and yew to the Mistress," replied Zethro. He motioned to Ann and Solomon to follow him as he began to make his way to Mistress Egypt. They followed. They made their way through the marshy land for about ten minutes when Zethro abruptly stopped and turned to the other two. "Miss Ann, youse know where we be rat now, does yew?" asked Zethro in a low voice.

"Yes."

Zethro then said, "Y'alls waits heer fur me to gib yew de signal to comes to the healing place." He then quickly turned and went forward along a trail in the marsh.

"We wait again," muttered Solomon impatiently.

"Hesh, voodoo mon," cautioned Ann in a concerned voice.

"You seem apprehensive, nervous," said Solomon. "Why? What is about to happen here?"

"Jist be patient, *mon cher*," put in Ann. "Mistress Egypt forseen dis meetin' a longs time ago, and she arrange it to her likin'. Jist yew wait."

"What did you say? She arranged all of this? It was not a chance sighting on the street in New Orleans? It was not coincidence that you and I met in Congo Square? Did she arrange for me to be given this gris-gris bag I have in my pocket?" asked Solomon impatiently amid the noises of the marshland.

"Gris-gris bag? What gris-gris bag?" asked Ann quickly and emphatically. "Where it be? Lets mc scc dat bag!"

Solomon pulled the gris-gris bag from his vest pocked and reluctantly handed it to the Cajun woman.

"*Sacre*! I tought dere be somtin bouts yew, voodoo mon."

152

As Solomon opened his mouth to ask what Ann meant, he heard extremely loud sound from the near distance. It seemed somewhat of a general moaning but yet incorporated a sense of happiness amid the sounds of the bayou.

"Dat's de signal froms Zethro for us to comes into de healin' place. Move it." Ann talked so fast it seemed she was mumbling to Solomon. He was unsure of what exactly the Cajun woman said so hastily and unclearly, but he recognized "signal" and "move" so he followed Ann. He was ready to meet Mistress Egypt.

As they moved forward along the little trail, he could see light from torches in the healing place. Dozens of them were stuck in the ground forming a large circle with many, perhaps a hundred or so, people thronged together with their backs to Ann and him as they entered the lighted area and made their way to the circle of torches. The people were silent, except for the crying of a couple of babies and the whining of several small children. Solomon also heard coughing and loud, wheezing breaths from the throng. Ann and he halted at the edge of the throng of people—black and white, young and old, men and women. Many appeared poor and ill. Solomon thought that most were here for whatever promise of healing the "healing place" promoted. "Some charlatans and snake oil purveyors must be here to prey upon the hopelessness of these people," Solomon thought to himself. "The poor people fooled by the hope of help from voodoo and such."

Ann softly said, "Now, voodoo mon, watch and wait for yer moment with Mistress Egypt." Solomon stood silently by the Cajun woman as they watched what was unfolding. The people, after hearing a voice make some sounds Solomon did not understand, sat en masse. Only Ann, Solomon, and a few others on the outside of the throng stood. Solomon was filled with anticipation.

Now he noticed three rather small constructed huts with roofs of palmetto fronds. Moss hung from various sections of the roof. Other ornaments and hides of animals had also been placed along the roof edges. Weeping willow branches leaned against the side walls of the huts. These huts were in front of the throng but outside the first circle of torches that brought immediate light to the healing place. There was an altar of sorts, covered with willow switches, inside the circle in front of the sitting people. Obviously, the people were waiting for someone or something to occur. The people basically remained quiet all this time.

At this moment Solomon observed that a large black man came from one of the huts, the nearest one to the throng of people. It was Zethro. He was wearing some sort of headdress on his head that covered his head but for his face. Out of the second nearest hut filed several women who wore skimpy clothes. Their hair was wildly sticking out from their heads. Their skin was painted with something white. They were chanting something.

Zethro reached the altar or table or whatever it was first. Amazingly, he stood upon it. The ten or twelve women now formed a line in front of Zethro. Music started playing from inside the two nearest huts. It continued for several minutes. It stopped. Then it began again. Now the white ghost-looking women began to dance and twirl. Solomon looked up at Zethro; he held some type of baton, flaming at both ends. He raised it to the moon and yelled several words at it. The women stopped their dancing and sat. Zethro ceased shouting at the moon but stood defiantly on the altar. He suddenly pointed to his right, and everyone looked upon two black women cutting the heads off two chickens each had held. The ghost-women all wailed up to the moon. Then suddenly they stopped. Zethro drew everyone's attention again with a strange sort of cawing noise directed to the moon and then dramatically pointed to his left. A huge bonfire was lit on the side where Zethro had pointed. It blazed up too quickly

154

it seemed. The flames seemed to reach up to the sky. Out from the bonfire it seemed stepped a redheaded woman. "It's Egypt!" exclaimed Solomon.

It was Egypt, but she was not covered completely by the gray cape with the black hood. The hood was down on the back of her shoulders, and the cape was not tied nor clutched to her body. She wore it open, showing a brilliant white robe-like dress. Now Zethro was beside her, taking the cape, as she stood, looking at the throng of people. The people stood and began chanting, "Egypt! Egypt! Egypt!" The chant increased in volume and enthusiasm, going on for a few seconds. Egypt bowed to the throng and turned to walk briskly back to the far hut. The crowd went silent and sat once more.

The ghost-like women walked among the people. Solomon could see women holding up babies, and men holding up their hands, palms out to the ghost-like women. He could hear pleading. The ghost-like women would gently tap a person on the head or touch the outward palm held up or daintily take a baby or small child from the arms of its mother. Adults and older children selected would be led by one of the ghost-like women to the entrance of the hut that Egypt had gone into a bit earlier. Infants and younger children would be picked up by the ghost-like women and carried to the hut entrance. No one could be observed coming out of the hut's entrance. A few minutes after a person had been taken to the hut entrance, those who accompanied them to the circle of torches would stand with outstretched arms toward the hut and then turn and leave the way Solomon and Ann had entered.

Solomon watched attentively to what was occurring. He turned to Ann to ask, "What is happening here?"

Ann replied, "Healin's."

"You mean these people come here to . . ."

Ann cut him off by saying, "Dey trusts Mistress Egypt and her magicals. Many been healed."

"But no one is coming out after they go in."

"De healed ones goes out de back of dat hut," Ann said. "If'n yew be watchin' some dese people froms de crowd, yew sees dat dey gets up to go and goes back de way we comes in. Look back at dat place over dere. See de ghosts womens reunites family rat dere at de edge of de light."

Solomon now watched behind them as well as look at the seated crowd and the ones escorted to the far hut. He could barely make things out, but he did see people waiting and reunited with family taken into the hut for Egypt to heal. Watching intently, he now could see happy faces and broad smiles when a mother and father were handed back a small child or infant.

"Mistress Egypt has healing powers? Really, she does?"

"Yew be rat," answered Ann.

"How many does she heal each time? How many times does she do this?"

"When de moon be full, Mistress Egypt does her good magicals. De number healed 'pend on her endurance at de time. Dere be no set number," answered Ann.

Solomon, about to ask more questions, now gave his attention to one of the ghost women who seemed to be approaching him. She did come directly through the seated crowd to directly in front of him. She held her arms out wide and then tapped him gently on the head with her right hand.

Ann crisply said to him, "Goes wid hur now, voodoo mon."

The woman grasped Solomon's right hand and pulled him through the mass of people on their way to the far hut. Solomon's

156

imagination was going wild. "What would this encounter be like? What would Egypt do to him? Did not she know he did not need healing? Why were they meeting like this? This way of meeting had already been predetermined? Was this encounter his destiny?"

The ghost-woman led him to the entrance of the hut. They paused for a few seconds. Solomon looked at the hut ornaments—animal skins, chicken claws, greenery, wind bangles, and what appeared to be dozens of gris-gris bags. He saw an alligator hide and a gator skull on each side of the entrance. And he noticed at the crown of the door frame a small bright metal object shaped like a pyramid. "One of those was what I had seen on Zethro's suspender strap," he thought, among all the other fantastic thoughts and images going through his head right now. The ghost woman parted the curtain of string beads for the two of them to enter. But it was not for the two of them to enter; the ghost-woman stood back a bit and shoved Solomon into the dimly lit hut. Solomon saw Mistress Egypt standing directly in front of him with Zethro slightly behind her to her right. She was beautiful, so beautiful. She smiled a mysterious smile at him. Solomon asked, "What kind of meet . . .?"

Before he could finish his question, Zethro bellowed, and Egypt raised her hand and blew a cloud of something aromatic about his head and face. Surprised, Solomon drew a quick, deep breath, and then he collapsed to the dirt floor.

He opened his eyes weakly but could not hold them open. He realized that Egypt had somehow drugged him. His mind was foggy. He remembered seeing and hearing things only randomly and incompletely—babies crying, walking with someone holding him upright, the lights and sounds of the river ferry, flickering light from the flames of the torches, and Egypt's smiling at him while reciting some incantation of sorts.

He awoke the next morning with the early sun shining on his face through the window on the east side of his room at the boarding house. He blinked his eyes several times to clear his vision. He raised himself a bit on the bed, but his head throbbed. "I have done it again," he thought. He went flat on the bed. He had on his same clothes from last night. He checked his pockets while lying flat. His derringer was still there. So was his wallet. So were a few loose coins. But the gris-gris bag was missing! He raised up his head and shoulders slowly. His head did not hurt the way it had a couple of minutes ago. He sat on the side of the bed. He checked the clock in the room. It was not even seven o'clock yet. He remembered the note he had left. He looked on the little table he had placed it on. It was gone, and in its place was a small piece of shiny metal in the shape of a pyramid with a small piece of paper under it. He pulled the note from under the pyramid-shaped piece of metal. It read, "Congo Square at noon. All your questions will be answered. Come alone." It was signed "Egiap."

Solomon washed and put on fresh, clean clothes and made it down to the boarding house breakfast of grits and bacon and biscuits. He ate heartily and talked with his friends about things in general but not about what he had experienced last night. He excused himself by saying he had banking business to attend to and went upstairs for a few minutes. He put the derringer into one of his vest pockets and wondered what had happened to the gris-gris bag. He put the written note in his wallet in his inside coat pocket. He went out of the boarding house into the city of New Orleans.

First, he went back to his bank to check if all was in order and his directives were on file and would be followed when he made purchases and other financial transactions. Then he visited the offices of Lawrence House and associates to confirm contacts in New Orleans, New York, and Richmond about purchasing and transporting slaves.

When he finished talking with Mr. House, a representative from his bank, and Mr. Huntington from the transportation company, Solomon, who had been watching the clock, knew it was time for him to walk to Congo Square for the meeting. While walking, he tried to remember some of the cloudy events of last night. He recalled hearing the chant of "Egypt! Egypt! Egypt!" again during the time he was drugged. He thought he remembered Zethro carrying him to the ferry landing and helping him walk onto the boat. Nothing else came to mind.

The day was bright, and the temperature comfortable at the time for him. He neared the entrance to Congo Square. "Caw! Caw! Caw! Caw!" came down from the top of one of the trees near the entrance. Some dogs barked nearby, and a cat screeched in the distance. "Why do I hear some of these same noises? Is that crow about again?" Solomon asked himself aloud as he glanced up toward where the sounds had originated. There was the strange hooded crow, turning its head from side to side observing all those who came its way. It fluttered its wings and lifted itself into the blue sky. It flew into the square the direction Solomon walked.

Solomon walked on and looked for the redheaded woman. He scanned all around with his eyes. Then he spotted her, sitting against the trunk of an old oak tree. Her gray cape with its black hood was on the ground beside her as well as what appeared to be a large covered basket of some sort. He noted that on the cape was a metal piece shaped like a pyramid. As he approached, the pyramid reflected the sun in his eyes for a brief instance. Egypt wore a blue long-sleeved dress that she had tucked under herself. She leaned back on the base of the tree and rested her arm on the basket. Solomon noticed that a bit past the tree loomed the presence of Zethro, who paced back and forth. "Mr. Witcher, please sit with me," said the redhead. "We have much to discuss, don't we?" She smiled that beguiling smile at him, and he returned one of his own. He sat.

159

"I assume you know my name because you went through my papers in my pockets?"

"That is how I became sure of it. I know many things about you, and I know very little about you," replied the redheaded woman. "But we will get to that in time."

"So what is your real name? Egypt? Egiap?" posed Solomon.

"They call me Egypt, but my actual name is Egiap. My last name is of little or no consequence, so you may call me Egiap, if you please," said the woman with a smile. She continued, "They dubbed me Egypt when most of those around here did not say my name correctly and corrupted it to Egypt because it sounded like that. And the connection with Egypt fits one of my Celtic legends. So I am known around here as Egypt. I took advantage of that and started wearing this pyramid to tie to the mysteries of ancient Egypt and thus increase awareness of me in order to help some of the people who had needs." She pointed to and touched the small pyramid pin attached to her collar. Solomon noted, too, that she was wearing some sort of heavy, decorative hairpins in the bun that she had fixed her bright auburn hair in to pull it up off her neck. The decorative ends reminded him of bent fingers holding fast to an object.

Solomon questioned, "What are those pins in your hair?" He pointed to the hairpins.

Egiap carefully pulled one of them from her red hair and held it out for Solomon to examine. He took it from her hand and rotated it to see the decorative finish of the polished brass hairpin. "That and the other one in my hair are really handpins to hold my cloak together. They are fasteners that I put to a second use to hold up my hair when it is off my neck."

"The design for each does resemble fingers of a hand holding or folding around something. I suppose that is why you call them

160

handpins," said Solomon as he continued to look at a designed symbol on one side of the decorative end. "Exactly what is this inscribed symbol?"

"That symbol is four interlocking shapes called *vesica piscis*; it protects the owner or one who wears or carries it.

"Protects from everything? A certain thing? Ill fortune?" inquired Solomon.

"Often after the time of the Roman Empire in Europe the *visica piscis* was a protection against witches. It was thought to be an anti-witch symbol."

"Oh," murmured Solomon slowly as he mused over the symbol on the handpin.

Egiap added, "Some thought it was used by witches as an aid in weather manipulation. Others thought it to be part of love charms."

"You certainly have me interested. Go on and tell me more," said Solomon in an uneasy voice.

Egiap continued, "God has awakened in me an energy, a power, an ability to soothe and heal and more. He has given me this knowledge that only a few individuals have been entrusted with and these abilities to manipulate energies around me and others."

"Are you a witch?" asked Solomon in a rather nervous tone. "What kind of question is that from a man whose last name is Witcher?" came back Egiap quickly. She laughed.

"Well, you got me there."

"Where did your last name come from?" asked Egiap. "You may have inherent qualities of a hexer imbedded in your soul."

"Oh, I doubt that it means much—probably a location where some of my ancestors lived some time or another," replied Solomon, trying to avoid clouded memories of Grandma Dundee's front porch sessions with the children and some not understood multiple confidences she whispered into his ear.

"Oh, so that is your belief?" said Egiap, half questioning and half matter-of-factly stating.

Solomon began to steer the conversation to find out what he wanted to know about this redheaded woman, "Ann told me that you have quite a knowledge of magicals, including voodoo, Amish witchery, and local hoodoo. Is what she said true?"

"Ann thinks she knows much more about me than she really does. But in plain and simple terms I am but a minion of the Lord— one who has strayed from the path at times and has an agenda of my own."

"What do you mean?"

"I am less than I seem and more than I seem," replied Egiap.

"Where are you from?"

"I was born and raised in Ireland and educated early on by my mother who had royal blood running through her veins."

"Are you Irish royalty?" asked Solomon. "Some of my ancestors came to this country from Ireland and Scotland. My Grandma Dundee said her mother was Irish and her father was Scottish. At least, that is what I remember. But I really know very little about our ancestors. Oh, and you just made plain to me that I was correct in thinking that you have more education than ordinary folks around here. And you do not have much of the Irish accent coming from the old country."

"My mother taught me early on that I needed to be able to speak in the old language as much as I could, that I needed to be able to speak in the Irish vernacular, and that I needed to be able to

162

converse without a heavy Irish accent. She often corrected me as we practiced each way," said Egiap.

"She instructed you well I think," added Solomon.

"I agree. Each way has served me well thus far in my life," said Egiap. "My mother taught me many other things early in my life, and she arranged for me to be instructed by some Druid practitioners, who showed me how to enhance the energies about me and surrounding others. They also taught me to pluck the strings of the timpan and use its music for my purposes. They instilled in me much Celtic lore, even that of ancient times of the Keltoi. They showed me the power of what the Romans named magic eggs made from serpentine that were used against evil incantations. They taught me about the *filidh*, the legendary poets of early Irish history. I even know some of the *ogham*, an alphabet used in the early times. They taught me the legendary connections with the ancient Egyptian pharaohs. I can tell you stories of dead kings and queens and many other things. I can tell you about gateways to other worlds. They made me aware of how special I am and how to harness and control certain forces in me and around me. They also swore me to an oath of helping others when appropriate to the time and situation. My oath included a vow of secrecy concerning the realm of my knowledge. I often wondered how my mother could pay for their teaching and mentoring of me until I overheard part of a conversation between two of them as I approached them at a nearby cairn where I always met them. The two ended their conversation abruptly when I appeared in front of them from the other side of the mound of stones. I heard something about blood flowing within my veins from Maeve of Connacht, who I found out later was a wicked queen. After that abrupt encounter, I never heard them say anything else about any queen from the past. I assume the Druid practitioners were indebted to my mother in some manner."

Solomon, fascinated by this revelation, asked, "Where were you born in Ireland?

163

"I was told that I was born at Visneach, located in the center of Ireland, and called Ireland's navel."

"How significant is that?" inquired Solomon.

"That I can not say. But I also know that my mother was born on an island in the middle of Lough Gur in Limerick."

"What is Lough Gur?"

"Lough Gur is a lake whose name means 'pain.'"

"Oh," breathed out Solomon. "That must imply something."

"Ah, yes, but that is another revelation for another day," said Egiap.

"How did you wind up in this country and down here in New Orleans?" asked Solomon.

"As a young one, my Druid mentors took me to touch the *Lia Fail*, the Stone of Destiny. Since that time I have allowed its power, aligned with that of God Almighty, to guide and direct me as to what I do and where I go," Egiap said.

"What gives you the direction? Are there signs or omens to guide you?"

"I trust a power inside me to guide me. It is not a voice. It is an intense feeling that results in a kind of intuition that is directive in nature. Several years ago when my mother died, I arranged passage on a vessel—one of the coffin ships—from Ireland to New York City. I felt as if I were directed by the power within me to travel there and then to join a band of Amish to settle in Pennsylvania.

"I saw an Amish couple once when my cousin Sawyer and I took off from school on a get-away trip to have some fun and to learn more about the different groups of Yankees in the North," added

Solomon. "Did you like the Amish? How were you accepted by them?"

Egiap continued, "They are a strict religious people. But they are welcoming once they know you and that you will try to blend into their society. After a couple of weeks within the group, an older woman took me aside and asked if I was a *braha*, a witch of sorts. We talked a long time that day. When we finished, she said we would talk again soon—with some others like her and me. We did so within a few days."

"What happened then?"

"I stayed with that group for a little over a year's time. They taught me much about the Amish *braha* practices. They were good *braha*, so-called white witches who worked in God's name, always giving God the glory for whatever good came out of their practices and lives. They would pull pain from those who hurt and those who were troubled. They used natural herbs, oils, spices, and spirituality to assist others and lift pain and trouble from them. But that comes at a price to the *braha*. The *braha* is a conduit for the hurt and bafflement. Evil energy goes into the *braha* and resides inside her until she can expel it through prayer and self-denial. I learned much from the *braha* practice that supported and enhanced my Celtic knowledge and skills."

"Then where did you go?" asked Solomon.

"I traveled to Cincinnati and took the river steamboats to Alexandria, Louisiana."

"Why there?"

"I was driven by the same inner force that brought me to America. I can not explain it or understand it, but I know I was to be there for a reason. And then when I traveled on the south side of the Red River to Avoyelles Parish, I encountered Ann at a cemetery. She

165

was the reason I was to be there at that place at that appointed time. She needed me, and I needed her. I traveled in Avoyelles Parish on my journey to New Orleans. But I must inject here that on my way down the Mississippi River from Cincinnati, the steamboat put in at Natchez, Mississippi."

Amazed at this statement, Solomon put in, "You went to Natchez?"

"Yes. It was appointed as well. When the riverboat stopped at Natchez, I had to disembark for a time while the men were unloading and loading cargo. At the landing I had enough time to walk up the hill to the top of the bluffs and look out upon the Mississippi River. It was a majestic view. As I stood overlooking the vast river and watched its currents carry driftwood and such downstream, I noted how hot the bright sun was and felt a bit overheated. I felt myself want to swoon but heard an old woman's voice speaking from behind me. I turned and saw this old, gray-haired, skinny woman wearing a faded yellow dress and carrying a wooden cup and a Bible that had a faded red string trailing from between its pages. She smiled at me and asked if I was too hot out here in the bright sun and if I needed a sip or two of water for relief. She handed me an old wooden cup with cool water in it. It had a minty taste. It was soothing just like her words were. We both sat down in the grass, and then she said to me, 'Yew must have faith in the Lord. Listen for the words from His Good Book and obey them. All yew need is faith the size of a single mustard seed.' She arose, smiled at me, and started walking the road back toward Natchez on the hill. I looked down and pondered what she said for just a very short time. When I looked up again to see her on the road, she was nowhere in sight."

Solomon looked intently at Egiap for a few seconds without saying anything. He felt a strange bond with her. Both had a shared experience with his Grandma Dundee, but he did not tell her who he thought the woman she met on the top of the hill was.

Now Egiap gave him one of her rather engaging smiles and said, "I have a confession to make to you."

"I know you are not a threat or danger to me because while I had you incapacitated in the hut across the Mississippi River, I performed the ritual known as *imbas forosna* to obtain 'the knowledge that enlightens,'" explained Egiap. "One of the things this ancient Celtic ritual can do is to find out if an individual harbors any kind of threat, danger, or ill omen to another. In a way it can see the future before it unfolds. Now I know that you can help me in my quest. I do not have to fear you in the least, even though you have certain, ah, abilities about you."

"I do not remember that ritual at all."

"Of course not," put in Egiap. "I was the nexus of the ritual. You had induced memory recollections, dreams, or nightmares that you can not remember now. Very few of the revelatory ones ever recall anything. You were not harmed physically. And only Ann and Zethro know about the ritual because they attended me during the time." Egiap continued, "At first all I knew was that something inside me guided me to come to the United States. Then, as time passed, I knew that I was guided to the Amish people to learn and enhance my abilities. I realized that I had not completed my journey for my destiny and traveled to Cincinnati to board a river steamboat to the town called Alexandria in Louisiana. I felt guided to leave the boat for a time in Natchez to go up to the top of the bluffs. When I reached Alexandria, I knew not why I was there and wandered for a short period of time until a dream sent me southeast to Avoyelles Parish."

Egiap paused for a moment, seemingly to reflect, and continued with her story, "It was there that I encountered Ann, and she accompanied me down river to New Orleans to see if this city was where I should be. I still was not sure if the city was my destination and calling until Ann and I were walking down Canal Street and came face-to-face with a Cajun man standing next to the wall of a building and spouting Scriptures and homilies about assistance to others. I was about to throw some coins into his old cap on the walkway when he shouted in a firm voice, 'Render therefore unto Caesar the things which are Caesar's; and unto God the things that are God's. Keep your coins. You will use them to help others in greater need than I. Go and heal! Use what God above has instilled in you. You may not slay the Yellow Jack, but you may avenge its scourge!'

"He smiled at me and repeated, 'Render therefore unto Caesar.' The man looked at me square in the eye which froze me in position momentarily. Then he reached and grabbed my right hand and placed seven red stones in it. 'These belong to you, my Irish lass. The largest and finest for you and the others for your devotees.' With those words he stooped to pick up his old cap, turned, and mingled with the crowd until he almost disappeared from our sight. The Cajun man suddenly whirled around and spoke in a very loud voice that could be heard over the street noise directly to me, 'But now thus saith the Lord that created thee, O'Suilleabhain , and he that formed thee, O'Suilleabhain, Fear not: for I have redeemed thee, I have called thee by thy name; thou are mine.'

"I suddenly was flushed with a general warm sensation that started in my right hand and flowed over my entire body, and tears came to my eyes. My mind traveled back in time to my training as a youth and made me think of that time my Druid teachers traveled with me to allow me to touch the *Lia Fail*. I experienced the same feeling then when I touched the Stone of Destiny with my right hand. Indeed, when the street preacher uttered 'O'Suilleabhain,' I felt that flood of warmth initiating in my right hand and streaming over my body and producing a wellspring of tears from my eyes. I knew at that moment that New Orleans was my destination but did not know the reasons yet. But one reason I ascribe to, because of that priest or brother, is that of healing of some of those in need."

"How do you know he is a brother or priest? A Catholic one or what?" asked Solomon, full of other questions as well. Solomon wanted to ask about that long word she said three times, but he was cut off by more information from Egiap.

"He must be! He had that air about him. He was obviously religious. He was inspiring. He was enlightening to me. Maybe this was an epiphany for me?" replied Egiap. "I keep repeating and reliving his words, trying to make some sense or sign from them or from his demeanor and appearance. But I have not done so yet."

"What did he look like? Describe his appearance to me."

"Yes, perhaps you can assist me in making additional sense of that meeting on the street," said Egiap. "The Cajun man was dressed . . ."

Solomon interrupted, "He was dressed in an old faded blue cotton shirt and old, torn blue trousers secured at the waist by an old piece of rope, wasn't he?"

"Yes, yes. That is exactly what he wore! How do you know" asked Egiap in disbelief.

"Because," replied Solomon, "I have met that man myself!"

Now it was Egiap's turn for wonderment. "I am simply amazed at what you are telling me. None of these meetings with that Cajun man were accidental. It must be God's work and His sign to me. We must determine what the sign is and what it means."

"Can you recall some of the Scriptures he was relating when you and Ann first approached where he was standing? Could there be something in those verses?" posed Solomon.

169

"I only remember these words that have lodged in my consciousness, 'Defend the poor and fatherless: do justice to the afflicted and needy. Deliver the poor and needy: rid them out of the hand of the wicked.'"

Just as Egiap said those Bible verses, Zethro approached them, saying, "Mistress Egypt, it be de time for yew to leave dis heer place."

Solomon rose to a standing position and was about to offer his hand to Egiap when she reached for the outstretched hand of Zethro. He easily assisted her to her feet. She smiled at Zethro and said, "Thank you." Zethro returned her smile and looked at Solomon in a condescending manner.

"When we will talk ag . . .

"Let us ponder what we have discussed and meet again here at noon in two days' time," said Egiap. She turned and began walking in the opposite direction of that from which Solomon had come. Zethro gave Solomon a rather stoic look and walked, following his mistress. Solomon watched them mix with other people and lost them in the crowd flowing in the other direction.

"Caw! Caw! Caw!" loudly cried a bird from the treetop where they had been talking. Solomon looked up to see it was the hooded crow. To Solomon the bird sounded condescending in tone. He watched as the bird took wing and flew in the direction that Egiap had walked. Solomon was perplexed. He turned to go back to the boarding house.

Solomon, during the interim between the two meetings, pondered the discussion, especially the Scriptures related by the Cajun man. Solomon thought there must be something, that sign Egiap sought, in those verses. He thought that perhaps Egiap and Ann had not heard enough of what that Cajun man was quoting. Maybe they had missed something or had not recalled everything quoted. As he

170

was falling asleep, he thought he would ask Mrs. Ducote tomorrow if he could borrow her Bible. He slept soundly.

The next morning after breakfast, Solomon inquired of Mrs. Ducote concerning her Bible. She immediately told him to go sit in the social-hour room to wait for her to go into her bedroom to get him her family Bible to read. She was pleased to hand the Bible to him. "Your personal guidance is in here, Mr. Witcher," she said assuringly to him.

She left Solomon alone in the social-hour room to read. He looked at Psalms and found the verses about defending the poor and delivering the poor and needy and removing them from the hand of the wicked. He looked at Matthew and read about the mustard seed his Grandma Dundee always spouted to the children on the porch. He turned pages, looking at various verses. Solomon lost track of time while searching the pages of Mrs. Ducote's family Bible.

By noon Solomon had given up, and he stopped to rest his eyes for a bit. He looked out the window at the passersby on the street. He thought about all that had happened in the last few days. He remembered his gris-gris bag was missing and wondered what he would do if it were not found. He thought about the old woman at THE MUSTARD SEED shop and consequences of not bringing the gris-gris bag back to her. Mrs. Ducote popped into the room and asked if he wanted to eat a simple mid-day meal with her. Solomon accepted her offer. The two conversed about the weather, local festivals, and the merits of running a boarding house in New Orleans.

Then Solomon went for a walk to get some fresh air and do some thinking about his future. He also thought about Egiap and what she was attempting to figure out as to what she was supposed to do here in New Orleans. His loss of the gris-gris bag kept recurring in his thoughts ever so often.

He walked and walked, reflecting upon the immediate past events. Before he knew it, he was at the entrance of Congo Square. He turned back and then continued walking while thinking. He could come to no resolution. He found himself near the coffee house where the private poker game took place. He felt an urge to go back there, to play more poker hands; but he resisted the feeling to go in and continued walking the busy streets. Now he thought about running into Ann or seeing Egiap again on the street.

He turned onto a busier street of walkers, horses, wagons, and riders. He stayed to the left side of the street and to the left side of the walkway in front of the storefront facades. The stream of walkers became denser and slower. The noise of the people and the street traffic became louder and more ominous. People were talking loudly and sometimes yelling. Wagon masters shouted at their draft animals and pedestrians that crossed too closely in front of them. But as Solomon made his way along with the stream of people, he began to discern one voice louder and stronger above all the other conversations and street noise. He could not make out what was being said, but the voice continued spouting words with only brief pauses. Now the voice was singing some kind of song—no, a chant! It was in Latin mostly. It was something about religious belief. Solomon moved closer to the source of the chanting.

The chanting suddenly ceased, and the strong, urgent voice returned to blast over the area of the street. The voice was one with a Cajun accent! It was spewing out Scriptures! Solomon purposely pushed his way through the throng of people surrounding the figure, which now he could make out. It was the Cajun man that had asked him for some coins the day he first saw Egiap and Ann. Solomon was so very curious as to what the man was preaching. He was now at the inner circle of the crowd, standing around the Cajun man. He wore the same clothes as the day Solomon had encountered him. He had the same look. Solomon spoke aloud, "What is the man saying?"

"Defend the poor and fatherless: do justice to the afflicted and needy. Deliver the poor and needy; rid them out of the hand of the wicked." The Cajun man ranted and railed in the vernacular and then quoted other Scripture.

Most of the onlookers were mesmerized. "Amen!" and "Praise the Lord!" were just two of the several remarks repeated by the standing onlookers.

A few of those who continued walking as they heard the street preacher yelled remarks of their own like "lunatic" and "crazy" and "get off the streets." Some even flung vulgarities at the man.

But those persons who stopped to listen were quite intent on hearing what the street preacher had to say. With the diversity of persons listening here on the New Orleans street, it was rather like Babel in reverse. Solomon could see a mix of people standing and listening. He could tell some of the onlookers were New Orleanians, some were Northerners, some were foreigners, some were Catholics, some were Protestants, some were black, some were sailors, some were poor, and some were rich.

Solomon began to fix his total attention on what the Cajun street preacher was preaching to his crowd on the street. He spewed forth words of sin and evilness, of justice and redemption, of Yellow Jack and punishment, of a coming conflict and individual personal sacrifice, of death and destruction, and of false pride and ruin. Solomon hung on each and every word because he thought that maybe some of what was being said had been said to Ann and Egiap and that they could piece together the sign or message Egiap sought.

Solomon listened carefully as Holy Scripture spewed forth from the Cajun man's mouth. "Defend the poor and fatherless: do justice to the afflicted and needy. Deliver the poor and needy; rid them out of the hand of the wicked," repeated the street preacher. "What does the Lord God have in store for you? Are you cleansed of your sins? Even if you do not die, there is a coming storm to punish you for your shortcomings! Examine your lives and your reasons for living. Prepare for God's damnation even in this earthly life! The Almighty will snuff out the lives of the wicked in this city like Sodom and Gommorah. Will you be one of the Lord's angels? Are you a servant of the Lord? I am a mere messenger trying to warn and direct you!" He continued but Solomon blocked out his immediate tirade, thinking about what he had already heard.

A loud "Amen" from the man standing by Solomon brought his attention back to the present. Now the street preacher was comparing God to a musician playing various instruments that were the people. His strong, loud words mentioned the lute, the harp, and the timpan. His rate of speech dropped.

"Will the music God finds in you be glorious?" said the preacher. His rate of speech became slower and more intensely emphatic, "But now thus saith the Lord that created thee, O Jacob, and he that formed thee, O Israel, Fear not: for I have redeemed thee, I have called thee by thy name; thou art mine."

When the Cajun man slowed his rate of words being delivered to the street crowd, he looked Solomon directly in his eyes and said at last, "Amen!" Some of the onlookers threw coins in the old cap at the man's feet before they departed. Other onlookers turned and walked away. Only Solomon remained.

"And what do you seek, young man?" said the Cajun man to Solomon.

"Meaning," replied Solomon.

"We all seek meaning for our lives. Even I, Xenophones, am seeking meaning for my own life," came back the Cajun man. "Seek your own personal epiphany. It will confront you when you least expect it. That is your quest," added Xenophones.

174

"But what do you mean, Xenoph-nophones?"

"Call me Xeno. I know that we have encountered each other before in this city. I feel that you are troubled by something inside you. May your epiphany occur before we encounter one another again," said Xenophones. Xeno picked up the coins at his feet in and around his old cap. He straightened up, held both his palms outward to Solomon and said, "Peace be with you, Brother!" Xeno disappeared into the crowd, leaving Solomon still perplexed.

Solomon turned himself and began walking back to the boarding house. He pondered all of what he had just heard with what Egiap had said. Back in his room he prepared to go down for the evening meal with the other boarders. He hoped that Herman Schmidt and Louis Bergeron would be there, for he could now discuss the Cajun man all of them had seen at different times. Both were there. He would broach the conversation with the news about Xeno at an appropriate break in dialogue.

The talk was about things in general and the deliciousness of the food for a time. Solomon was just about to talk about Xeno when Louis said to Solomon, "Remember the Cajun man Herman and I saw at Congo Square while you were not with us?"

Solomon nodded in affirmation.

Herman said, "What of him?"

"Well, I was curious, so curious about the delightfully different individual that I inquired of several of my friends and fellows about the Cajun man. I found out that his name is . . ."

"Xenophones," interjected Solomon.

"Why, yes. How do you know?" asked Louis. "I encountered him on the street, preaching away at all of us sinners," replied Solomon. "But I know little of him other than his name."

175

"Ah, my friend, I can tell you more about this street preacher. I have heard much, but I how much of what I have heard is true, I do not know."

Herman put in, "Tell us what you heard—hearsay or no."

Louis continued, "Xenophones is the son of Jules and Bernadette Picard, both deceased as a result of the 1853 yellow fever epidemic here in New Orleans. All other members of Xeno's family, younger sister and two younger brothers, died from the fever as well. The family was well off—rich by most people's standards. They had a large house and extensive property in a good part of the city. The fever had afflicted Xeno as well, but he survived the malady. It is said that he became bitter and questioned everything including God. He sold all his property and gave most of the money to charity and the poor in the city. His anger festered in him for over a year. He drank the rest of the money away in his anger and sorrow. Only his family priest, Father Ones, could talk with Xeno and hold his confidence during the roughest time, right after Xeno recovered and his other family members did not. Father Ones had a terrible time trying to keep Xeno in the faith and preventing him from doing only God knows what. Father Ones, as the story goes, was able to help Xeno through his perceived hell on earth by taking him into the slave pens of the city's slave trade."

"I have never been to see any of the slave markets or slave pens. Have you seen the slave market on Esplanade and the river?" asked Herman. "I heard it has terrible conditions for the slaves to be sold."

Louis answered, "I have been there once with some friends from out of town when one wanted to purchase a house servant. The Theophilus Freeman slave pen and market is, indeed, horrible. The conditions are not suited for humans—slaves or not. This aspect of the whole business of slavery is abominable and inhumane. But the

176

slaves do get some good treatment when they are prepared for auction. They are given some clean clothing and the opportunity to wash up. Of course, all this is preparation for their being sold. But nothing diminishes the ill treatment most of the slaves suffer at all other times. I saw men and women kicked and beaten and called animals and scum and all such other vulgarities that one can imagine. They were made to dance and prance about and cautioned to remain in their proper places. At the auction I attended with friends, we saw mothers and children separated at the sale. Before the sale of a certain lot of slaves occurred, we went through other parts of the slave pens where both men and women slaves were stripped for inspection in front of both men and women buyers. Some of the holding pens had this stench about them that I could not forget the smell for months after the visit. That stench stayed in my clothes I wore that day for weeks, even though the clothes were washed several times. These inner pens and cells were all dank and musty and reeking of that unimaginable stench. How those slaves placed there could even breath, I do not know. I saw some slaves who were labeled as trouble who had old scars and new lash wounds on their backs and shoulders. Many had green infection with open sores. Both men and women had little, if any, dirty clothing to cover their bodies. I shall never forget the one slave I observed sitting in the dirty, smelly back corner of one of those single cells. She knelt in the middle of the single cell holding pen and looked straight out its front. We passed there several times, and the slave woman was in the exact same position. All the while she stared with fiery eyes straight ahead of her. Each time we passed I could see the hatred and anger and defiance in her eyes. She seemed to seeth with those passions, but she did not move or utter a single sound. She was like a fixture there. That slave woman, along with the stench of that place is forever etched in my nostrils and my mind's eye. I never want to go back to that establishment again. The only thing I would want to take from that place is that black slave woman's defiance."

177

"Father Ones used the horrible conditions that Xenophones saw to guide him into the initial steps of the priesthood. Xeno stayed with the process and training up until the last vow that would consecrate him into the priesthood. After several years of training and education, Xeno suddenly balked and informed Father Ones of his decision. Xeno made his case with the proper Catholic officials, and they gave their blessings to him to walk away from the rites and the rituals to go about his secular life. Xenophones disappeared from society and the New Orleans scene until one day last year he was seen preaching on the city streets. No one knows where he had been or why he is now on the streets proclaiming whatever it is he is proclaiming."

"Poor man," said Herman Schmidt. "What he endured probably would have broken me as an individual."

"Was there any other information about him?" asked Solomon.

"The word on the streets is that he is often seen helping poor families with little gifts of money he gets preaching, assisting old people with fixing up their houses, aiding other street people to find shelter, volunteering at the Charity Hospital, and even performing Shakespearean scenes on street corners. There are some other wild stories like his roaming the Girod Street Cemetery—where all his family was entombed—in the middle of the night and during the day frightening children by swallowing small dogs and cats whole in front of them. But those last two examples are hard to justify when all the others are examined. Who really knows?" said Louis Bergeron.

"He is some character I say. Just from what we saw of him in Congo Square," added Herman. "His name is unusual, to say the least. How did it come about?"

"His family was well-educated, including his mother. Mrs. Bernadette loved the ancient Greeks. She named him Xenophones

178

after the Greek philosopher-poet. His full name is Jules Xenophones Rabalais Picard."

"You said you saw him and experienced some of his street preaching?" asked Louis of Solomon. "What did you observe?"

"I walked up on him addressing a small throng of people," replied Solomon.

"What was he saying? What was the topic of his preaching?" asked Herman.

"Defend the poor and fatherless: do justice to the afflicted and needy. Deliver the poor and needy; rid them out of the hand of the wicked," answered Solomon.

"That's from the book of Psalms," injected Mrs. Ducote, who was removing some dishes from the table by them.

"Yes," said Solomon. "A friend of mine and I are attempting to determine the exact message he is sending out to the streets upon an almost daily basis. We are having little luck. We agreed that he is declaring that something bad will occur—some kind of massive conflict."

Mrs. Ducote put in, "I may jist have to find this street preacher and hear what he has to say."

The conversation drifted to other matters of routine and to the hot weather. At the end of the meal, all bid one another a pleasant night and good rest. Solomon fell asleep relatively easily and awoke refreshed in the morning.

Today Solomon went to the bank to discuss business and arrange passage to New York City to pursue his business interest there. It took him the greater part of the day to attend to all his business. He would leave for the North in a few weeks to seek his fortune. He walked a roundabout way to get to the boarding house. He had hoped

179

he would see Ann or Egiap or even Zethro. He thought about the gris-gris bag he owed the old woman at THE MUSTARD SEED and consequences, if any, that would play out in his life. He decided that he should go back to the gathering and poker game at the coffee house several times before he would leave for New York City. He could win some extra money to give to the old woman in lieu of the gris-gris bag or purchase her a custom-made one to suit her purposes. He made it back to Mrs. Ducote's boarding house in time for the evening meal.

The next morning he was primed to meet with Egiap again at noon in the park. Perhaps she had divined what she required from the Scriptures. He was at a good distance from the meeting point when he heard the familiar cawing of that pesky hooded crow and noticed that its shadow passed on the ground from behind him going toward the meeting tree. "Is that bird a curse on me? Is it some kind of omen for me?" he thought out loud. He glanced up from the ground in front of him to see a figure sitting beneath the tree and another pacing back and forth behind it. Egiap and Zethro were already there. He walked quickly forward toward them. Zethro spied Solomon before Egiap did. He moved up beside her under the tree.

Just as Solomon reached the shade of the tree, Zethro said, "Hello, Massa Witcher, mistress been waitin' for yew." He turned and walked away to the same general area he paced back and forth the last time Egiap and Solomon had talked. He took his job of being Egiap's bodyguard very seriously. He watched them and observed all who approached the area. He was obviously quite devoted to her.

"Solomon, how nice to see you today!" said Egiap. "Have you thought much about our discussion and that man preaching in the streets?"

"Yes, most extensively," replied Solomon. "And I saw him and listened to him since we met. I think I heard about the same Bible

180

verses and admonitions that you did—except maybe that I overheard more of his religious ranting."

"You did see and hear him! Why, that should aid very much in our thinking to determine the message and perhaps my personal direction," Egiap said.

Solomon sat on the ground in the shade just in front of Egiap. He saw out of the corner of his eye that Zethro was watching as he did so. Solomon now decided to get some information about Zethro to satisfy his own curiosity about the devotion to Egiap. Solomon asked, "Before we talk about the street preacher, please answer a couple of questions about your man Zethro. Exactly who is he, and how did he get into your service? Is he your personal slave?"

Egiap immediately and emphatically stated, "Zethro is not anyone's slave! Not anymore!"

Solomon remained silent. Egiap stared coldly at him and said, "You want to know about Zethro? I will call him over so you can hear his story first-hand." With those words Egiap said in a loud voice, "My Zethro, please come over here." She waved him over to where they were sitting in the shade beneath the tree.

Zethro came over slowly.

"Please sit with us for a time," said Egiap as she patted the ground next to her for Zethro to sit. "Mr. Witcher is interested in you and your background. Let's take a bit of time to inform him and answer any questions he has, OK? He wants to know about how the two of us met and how you chose to accompany me."

"Yea, mistress. I be willin' to tells Mr. Witcher 'bout me when de grim reaper almost tooks innocent me and dat Mistress Egypt save me from de grave. Since den, I's be beholden to Mistress Egypt and wants to serves her in what it be she wish."

"She saved you from death?" asked Solomon.

181

"Yew be rat," replied Zethro.

"Go ahead to tell Mr. Witcher, Zethro. He really wants to know," said Egiap. "I will preface what you say with the meaning of your old African name. Zethro means 'born innocent.' An old slave woman that I helped told me what his name means at a healing one night when I had called his name in her presence."

Zethro looked at Egiap. She nodded her head and smiled at him. "Please start with the time your last master purchased you here in New Orleans just before your poor mother passed."

He began, "Massa Barilleaux boughts me frum my sick mama when I's wuz littler den a hitchin' rail. He tought dat I grows up bigger and strong and useful tos hem. But I's be some slow in thinkin' stuff. Dis makes Massa Barilleaux gits angry wit mees. He hits mees in de hed wit him fine walkin' cane all de times I's too slow fer him. He call me 'dumb darkey' and 'stupid nigger' alls de time," Zethro halted for a minute.

"Go ahead, my Zethro. You tell Mr. Witcher all," put in Egiap.

"Sometime Massa Barilleaux gits me whupped at de big house whens I's slow in mees thinkin'. He laughs when de knotty whup larrups and cuts up my back. I gits by de hurt cuz I tink dats wat happen to Jesus."

"His back is covered by scars from the lash. He is so innocent about worldly matters," added Egiap. "He is so innocent." Solomon saw tears forming in her eyes as she spoke.

"Buts Mistress Egypt claimed me on de street one day some summers ago. Massa Barilleaux struck mees with dat cane. Please, Mistress, wills yew tells de rest of whats happen dat day?

"Yes, Zethro, I will finish the story," replied Egiap. "That ungodly man was about to beat innocent Zethro again on the street. I had been walking toward them and saw the entire episode. I knew

182

that I must stop it and claim Zethro. I advanced to a couple of feet in front of Barilleaux and demanded that he stop. We had words, unpleasant words. Of course, he became angry and cursed at me and drew his hand holding the cane back to strike me. Zethro had picked himself up and was about to grab Barilleaux's arm when I stopped Barilleaux's action with an enchantment imbedded in my own gris-gris bag and force of mind. Barilleaux dropped his hand and his cane to the board walk and just looked at me in disbelief. I told him that I would purchase Zethro for a fair price. In his stupor he agreed to the purchase if I could bring $500 to the coffee house at the intersection of Bienville and Bourbon streets by three o'clock the next afternoon. I secured the money and went to the appointed meeting place about a half hour before the designated time."

"Was he there?" asked Solomon.

"He was. But not Zethro," replied Egiap.

"Where was he?"

Egiap continued, "Barilleaux had sold him and placed him down at the slave market and Theophilus Freeman's slave pens. When he informed me of where I would have to go to buy Zethro, he laughed out loud in a wicked, maniacal sound. He hit the bar with that walking cane of his and laughed again. Then he became quiet and motioned me over closer to him. I moved only a bit closer. He, now in a quieter voice, said that I was such a lovely woman and he could help me retrieve Zethro from the slave pens if I would be nice to him in a room upstairs. He smiled an arrogant smile at me and laughed quietly. He stepped toward me, and I immediately stepped backward. I told him that he did not know who he was messing with and to beware this Irish bansee if he were any kind of smart. I turned and walked away as he laughed out loud again. I can still hear that ugly laugh echoing in my mind."

"Did you go to the slave market?"

183

"Yes, I did so upon leaving the establishment. I wondered if I would have enough money to purchase Zethro now since he had just been sold by Barilleaux. I stood outside in front of the slave pens for a time just looking at the people flowing in and out. The slaves were treated like animals and marched in, sometimes in coffles. I heard cursing and the lash of whips striking human flesh. I was horrified as I entered the building area. It was dank and musty-smelling. I made my way to a person that seemed to be in charge of an area and inquired of a slave named Zethro that had been brought in yesterday or today. He directed me to some inside location that had desks and seemed to be office areas. I asked ten or twelve men about Zethro. No one could tell me anything until I off-handedly stated to one man that Zethro was a young man that was slow to understand and probably be considered resistant to authority. That man looked up thoughtfully and sent me to an area of single cells. Hurriedly I looked in each one until I saw Zethro curled up in a corner. His shirt had been ripped to shreds by a whipping or two, and his back was bloody and swollen and cut in crisscross manner. He hid his head in his hands and was moaning quite loudly. No one noticed or cared. He was considered a discard, and it was no telling what may have been done with him. I started asking every well-dressed man that passed me where I could buy the slave in the single cell at the end of the row. After two hours I finally talked with the right person and made arrangements to purchase Zethro and take him out of that hell hole. The asking price for Zethro was $600, but I talked the trader down by emphasizing Zethro's shortcomings and attitude toward being bossed about. At one point I was asked why I wanted the worthless, obstinate slave. I told the trader that he once belonged to my sister and that she felt sorry for him because of his slow mind. I said that our father sold him away because we were leaving New Orleans for Europe. I said that my sister had found a kind master in the city for Zethro to serve in his limited capacity. The trader took me to one of the desks, filled out some papers, kept several pages, and in return for the cash gave me ownership papers for Zethro. Then it took another hour for them to bring Zethro to me. Zethro, at first, did not know what was happening to him and had to be dragged to me by four burly men. When he saw me, his eyes lit up, and he recognized me as the woman who had intervened with Barilleaux on the street. He stopped resisting the men. They let go of him and pushed him over toward me. We left immediately for me to tend to his back and shoulders."

Zethro added, "Mistress Egypt claim me frum de devil. I's be thinkin' dat day in slave pens I's gonna die. Den she tells me dat I be a free man and show de papers to me wit my name on dem. I's thanks hur and will serve hur til de day I be ded."

"You do have a devotee in Zethro," said Solomon. "I have another question for you, Egiap. This name Egiap, did your mother in Ireland give it to you?"

"No, the old Druids called me Egiap," replied she.

"Do you know why this name was bestowed upon you?"

Egiap answered, "I believe the name was derived by the Druid practitioners from the stars' and planets' location in the sky the night I was born. There is some kind of relationship with the study of numbers and numerical systems traced back as far as the early Celts and ancient Egyptians as well, but no one ever enlightened me of any name sake."

"But what is your real name, your birth name?"

"The Druid practitioners were always around as long as I can remember. I think they observed me as I grew from a helpless infant into a walking, talking little girl. They were not always directly in my life, but they were forever lurking in the perimeters of what happened as I grew. And then they were my teachers for much of each day. They always called me Egiap. So that is who I am and ever will be. I hardly remember being addressed by any other name," she said and

185

paused, seemingly to muse over what she had just said. Then she said, "Now let us go back to what the street preacher was declaring to all of us."

Egiap looked at Zethro kindly and said in a pleasant voice, "I know you feel more at ease pacing over there and observing us and watching over us from that little distance. You may go if you wish."

"Yus, Mistress Egypt. Mys job be to protect yew," replied Zethro. Egiap smiled at him and touched him on the shoulder as he arose.

"What Scriptural verses or phrases do you recall the most?" asked Egiap of Solomon.

"Defend the poor and fatherless: do justice to the afflicted and needy. Deliver the poor and needy; rid them out of the hand of the wicked."

"Anything else?" asked Egiap.

"But now thus saith the Lord that created thee, O Jacob, and he that formed thee, O Israel, Fear not: for I have redeemed thee, I have called thee by thy name; thou are mine."

"Any other?" asked Egiap once more.

"No. No other Bible verse, but he did say that musical instrument that you said you could play—that old, ancient Celtic one, the tinpam, the timpal—now what was it?"

"The timpan is its name." Egiap paused for a moment. "He actually said timpan?"

"Yes. Yes. He did. I remember it distinctly because I remembered you telling me about being able to play it. He said something about each of us being a musical instrument played by God Himself. Is that important?"

"It may be significant," answered Egiap. Then she said, "Let us meditate for a few minutes." She closed her eyes.

Solomon looked at her and then at Zethro in the background. He, too, closed his eyes to think. He focused on the task and felt a sense of energy about himself. He opened his eyes to see Egiap. She seemed to have an aura about her. Now she began to hum in a low, low tone. Solomon shut his eyes once more and concentrated. He thought he now felt a synergy with Egiap. It was a soothing feeling of warmth and comfort.

He was pulled from his cocoon of synergy by Egiap's sudden, loud words, "I have it. I have determined the message and my purpose for being here in New Orleans!"

Solomon, now suddenly uneasy, said, "Tell me. Tell me. What must I do to assist you?"

"It was not coincidental that I was the one to confront Barilleaux on the street when he was beating Zethro. In my brief time with him I could tell what kind of person he is in deep inside his soul. I also learned that he is one of the leaders of New Orleans business men and newspapermen that held back knowledge of the 1853 yellow fever epidemic that swept the city. The rich are always able to move out of the city when a dire illness is spreading through the population. The poor rarely can do the same but must endure the sickness as it spreads by taking other measures. The 1853 epidemic hurt my people, the Irish, much harder than in the past because of their living conditions and the severity of the yellow fever. So many Irish and others died needlessly because the business men like Barilleaux cared more about lack of possible profits from New Orleans being quarantined by other ports and shipping areas. Justice must be served on Barilleaux, the main leader of holding back yellow fever news and announcements. I am here to effect justice for the epidemic and for all those born innocent like Zethro. I have been called by name."

Solomon, still uneasy, could not find words to say anything for a few moments. Before he could say anything, Egiap said, "You know this man Barilleaux? You have associated with him, have you not?"

"I—I don't remember. Have I?"

"Think, Solomon. Who have you seen with a fine walking cane? When we were meditating, I felt that Barilleaux's essence had brushed up against yours at one time or another while you were here in New Orleans. Focus your mind," she stated.

Solomon did as Egiap said. He closed his eyes and thought about men he had met or seen with walking canes. There was the boarder with the cane encasing a knife or dagger. There was the Mexican War soldier with the bum leg in one of the bars he had visited. And then there was the man Jim at the poker game gathering that he first played in. Jim had picked up a fine walking cane as he left that night. And his last name was, indeed, Barilleaux. Solomon opened his eyes and affirmed what Egiap had surmised.

Egiap now spoke, "The next full moon will dictate our timing, but here is what we shall do . . . . "

Solomon frequented the coffee house for many nights, hoping Barilleaux would be there in the game each evening. One night James Barilleaux was there. Solomon attempted to get re-acquainted with Barilleaux and to study the way he played cards, the way he acted when around just the men, the way he acted around the woman at the gathering, and what seemed to needle him or upset him.

Solomon received a message from Egiap at the boarding house that the next full moon would begin in three nights. She also told him how to contact her when Barilleaux would next be at the poker gathering to set the plan into action. Barilleaux played one night, won big, and told the other players to bring more money to the next night's game for him to win because he was returning with all his good luck.

188

Solomon sent his message to Egiap that night. All the arrangements had been completed. Ann was to be at the coffee house in the afternoon to meet Solomon at two o'clock when he would pay his admission ante.

That night Solomon arrived at the coffee house a few minutes after nine p. m. as he usually did. He spoke to Babineaux and to Sisera, who escorted him upstairs as usual. He greeted Ramley at the doorway to the gathering room. Sisera held his arm as they walked through the double doorway. Solomon was already seeing who is in the room, especially at the poker table. James Barilleaux and Gaston Dubroc were at the table, playing a hand of cards with others Solomon did not know. The table was full, except for his chair. Bartholomew greeted Solomon Witcher as usual and changed his money for poker chips. Solomon recognized two of the women sitting near the food and drink table and knew one other—Ann. Ann was dressed better than he had ever seen her. Her hair was combed and fashioned beautifully. He had not realized before this moment how lovely she was. The necklace she wore had a beautiful cork red stone as a pendant. She even looked more alluring than the usual women there. She seemed to ignore his long stare and did not acknowledge his continuous glances in her direction.

The game carried on after Solomon took his chair and dealt his first hand of cards for the evening. The big winner continued to be Barilleaux. At the break for food and drink Barilleaux, as usual, headed for the green absinthe drinks. Before he could reach the table where the green drinks were, Ann was there to pick up a glass and carefully hand it to Barilleaux. She smiled up at him with an inviting look and grasped his arm, talking to him in a lively manner. He sipped the glass after removing the fork and conversed with her, taking several more sips of the green liquid. Then the two of them sat at the near table. Ann laughed out loud at Barilleaux's jokes and kept leaning forward toward him. It became obvious to all in the room that

Barilleaux was most interested in what Ann's low-cut dress revealed to him each time she leaned toward him. Other regular poker players had never seen or heard Barilleaux this loud and vocal with any of the other girls. He had sat and talked and drank with many of them, but tonight it was as if he were in a playful mood and had left his inhibitions downstairs when he came in. Ann flirted and more with him almost endlessly at the break in the game.

When called back to the cards at the end of the break, Ann passed close to Solomon and said in a low voice, "Dat philter charm I slipped in his drink is workin'. Now de actin's up to yew. We women be back in an hour." Solomon watched as Ann went to speak a few words with Barilleaux before she left the room. Barilleaux slapped her on the rump as she left him.

The card game resumed. But now Barilleaux was not winning as he had done before the break and the previous evening. He continued to be loud and arrogant. Solomon really concentrated on each individual hand of the poker game. He also focused segments of his attention on the other players, particularly Barilleaux, in order to read each players' individual poker face. Solomon began a winning streak, usually throwing down the winning hand in Barilleaux's face when Barilleaux was sure he had the winning hand. Barilleaux now became louder at the loss of each respective hand. He began sending ungentlemanly remarks and then outright insults toward Solomon and other players. But because Solomon was winning the most hands, most of the insults were aimed at Solomon. All other players could see that Barilleaux was festering with anger at Solomon more and more as the game progressed with Solomon's winning streak more or less intact. Barilleaux pounded on the table with each of his lost pots from the hands. He cursed loudly.

At this point the women entered the room once more. They circled the table and players with Ann touching Barilleaux on the shoulder as she went by him to stand behind Solomon. A hand was dealt by Gaston and the betting began. Barilleaux seemed to lose interest in the card game and focus his attention on Ann who was standing behind Solomon. Ann noticed his hard glances at Solomon. Now Ann placed her hands on Solomon's shoulders and leaned down to whisper into his ear. Solomon nodded and turned his head to smile up at her.

Barilleaux suddenly exploded in anger, yelling at Solomon. Barilleaux stood up and directed more cursing toward Solomon, all the while warning him to let Ann be. Solomon knew to feed the green-eyed monster, so he reached his right hand up to cover Ann's hand still on his shoulder. "Witcher!! Witcher!!" yelled Barilleaux.

"Mr. Barilleaux!" called out Bartholomew louder than Barilleaux had yelled. "You will restrain yourself in this establishment. This game is a gentlemen's game. Behavior of this nature shall not be tolerated." Bartholomew pulled a hand bell from his pocket and shook it producing a shrill clanging tone. Ramley entered the room from outside in the hall.

Now Solomon stood, and Ann moved by his side, grasping his arm and clinging as much as possible to him.

"Mr. Solomon Witcher, yew are a damned scoundrel and crooked manipulator of the cards! Admit that yew are a common cheat in this gathering! And how did yew enchant that woman into leaving my companionship this night? Yew shame me!" Barilleaux said loudly and firmly.

"Mr. Barilleax, you have quite overplayed your luck at cards and women tonight," said Solomon calmly.

"Yew foul my good name and cause me shame when yew utter my good name," replied Barilleaux. "I call yew out for my personal satisfaction!"

191

Bartholomew injected, "Are you, Mr. Barilleaux, challenging Mr. Witcher to a formal duel in front of this company of individuals? Is that what you are doing?"

Before Barilleaux could say anything, Solomon spoke in a quiet, calm voice saying, "Before he can mince words, I hereby challenge Mr. Barilleaux to a duel. Please name the weapons so that I can call the place and time of your demise!"

Without hesitation Barilleaux said, "Single shot pistols. I have a matched pair, and yew may select the one yew want first."

"Call the location and time, Mr. Witcher," said Bartholomew mechanically.

"Three hours from now at the Girod Street Cemetery," said Solomon plainly and without emotion.

Barilleaux blanched momentarily and then stoically said, "So be it!"

"Because the disagreement began here, Ramley and I shall attend the duel and be its directors. I shall inspect the pistols before the count and pacing," said Bartholomew to each of the gentlemen who were involved. "Bring along one person for your second. I shall fetch a doctor along as well. May God have mercy on the two of you."

Solomon remained calm and stood in place with Ann holding onto his arm, still clinging to him.

Barilleaux stormed angrily out of the room with Ramley following slightly behind to ensure his departure from the establishment.

Ann let go of Solomon's arm and quietly said, "It worked."

"Now let's find Egiap and proceed to the cemetery. The others will congregate at the entrance in about an hour," said Solomon. They went downstairs and then departed the building in single file, not talking but only thinking about what was to come.

Solomon and Ann met Zethro just down the street from the cemetery. He informed them that Egiap was already in the cemetery near the societies' tombs area. He also told them that he had scouted the whole cemetery before as she was meditating or praying at the entrance under the Death's Head monument. He wanted to hurry back to the section his mistress was in. But Zethro walked with Ann and Solomon and did not leave them until they all arrived at the entrance to the cemetery and stopped to gaze upward at the Angelica Dow monument, which had a rather cubical base with an obelisk atop that had a skull's face with two crossed bones beneath it. Also, on the front a little more than halfway up was an oval with the year "1822" in it in raised letters. The monument was commonly known as the Death's Head monument. In an instant Zethro said, "That is the way!" as he pointed and disappeared into the cemetery out of the light from the street.

Ann looked up at the skull face and bones and said to Solomon, "*Mon cher*, dis be de creepiest spot on de gud Lord's earth! Me, I gots de scares in dis place rat here. I tink dat de skull gonna git some eyeballs and puts some of dat ole evil eye on me and yew! Buts Mistress Egypt done tole me to place dis here on de monument on de front ledge 'neath the Death Head."

Ann moved forward and placed an object on the monument. Solomon could not make out what the object was and was about to look more closely at it. Ann grabbed his hand and pulled him toward the direction they should go in. Just before they departed the monument, they heard a cawing from above them. There perched on the topmost part was the hooded crow. It looked at the two of them, cawed loudly three times, and flew in the direction taken by Zethro.

193

The two of them walked the direction Zethro had pointed out. At the second step into the darkness of the cemetery, Ann reached out and grasped Solomon's arm. He heard her inhale deeply. In the wide center aisle they saw Zethro with a flambeaux lighting another torch and then others arranged on each side of the aisle. Now this area the cemetery was ablaze with light from the torches, and eerie shadows danced on the sides of the tombs outside the lighted area. Ann let go of Solomon's arm as soon as she saw Egiap.

Egiap motioned Ann over to the side, where Ann stood silently. Solomon went to stand by Egiap. Egiap said in a low tone, "I am your second for this event this evening." Solomon said nothing but turned as soon as he saw and heard Zethro running into the lighted area toward them.

Zethro ran up to his mistress and said, "Dey be comin', Mistress. It be all of dem." Egiap nodded her head and simply responded in a quiet voice, "Thank you, my Zethro."

Egiap spoke again in a low tone to Solomon, "As I said, I am your second for your duel with Barilleaux, but you will not shoot him. I will end his evilness." She reached inside her cloak and pulled out Solomon's missing ivory-handle dagger and flashed it in his field of vision.

All—Barilleaux, his second, Ramley, Bartholomew, and a physician—walked into the lighted area. Solomon and Egiap move toward the middle of the lighted lane there in the Girod Street Cemetery. Introductions were formally made. The doctor's name was Alton Landrieux, and Barilleaux's second was an older man named Percival Knight.

Barilleaux opened a dueling pistol case with two rather new-looking matched pistols set into the recessed areas designed for them. He handed the case with the pistols to Bartholomew without saying any words. Barilleaux had a rather grim yet determined look upon his face.

Bartholomew examined the pistols and then handed them to Ramley, instructing him to load each. The full moon popped out from behind the clouds and illuminated the section of the cemetery even brighter than the torches alone.

Now in the moonlight and the torchlight, Barilleaux stared intently at Solomon's second as she pushed back her cloak's hood from her head. "My God! It's yew!"

Egiap smiled at him, pointed over to Zethro, and replied, "And that is Zethro."

"What does all of this mean?" cried out Barilleau. He raised his walking cane high in the air. Some of the flames from the torches reflected their light on the fine silver gilding the top of the cane. He received no answer of his question and lowered the cane back to its normal position he held it in when standing.

Now all the clouds that had cluttered the night sky had been blown to the east by the easy winds that night. The full moon seemed larger and brighter than it had been a couple of hours ago. Still the flaming torches cast disturbing shadows on the tombs. The shadows seemed to be frightened of themselves and flickered here and there, seemingly playing an eerie game of hide-and-seek.

There was silence for a few moments longer until Bartholomew spoke. "Ramley, are the pistols properly loaded?"

Ramley stated the affirmative and handed a loaded pistol to Barilleaux and to Solomon, who had moved directly in front of Bartholomew. The two duelists inspected the pistols. "Are the pistols ready? Are the duelists ready?"

Barilleaux and Solomon nodded in agreement.

Bartholomew now directed the two men to opposite ends of the torch-lit avenue in the lane of the cemetery. He spoke coldly, "Our establishment ascribes to the dueling code that allows both participants to shoot once and calls for the duel to be considered done if blood ensues from either of those shots. If the duelist who challenged the other formally says his honor is restored and wants to end the duel, thus it be so. Otherwise, the duelists will have the pistols reloaded and will have the experience of shooting again until blood or reconciliation occurs. Are there any questions, gentlemen?"

Both men remained silent.

"Now, each of you go to an opposite end of the lighted area. I will instruct each of you to take ten paces upon my count toward your antagonist. At that point watch for the drop of my hat from my outstretched arm. When the hat begins to fall, you may take aim and discharge the pistol at your adversary. Am I clear, gentlemen?"

Both of the men said "yes" aloud and moved to an end of the lighted avenue.

The men turned to face one another. Both held their pistols in their right hands about shoulder high with the barrels pointed upward.

Bartholomew began his count, "One . . . two . . . three . . . four . . . five . . . six . . . seven. . . eight . . . nine . . . ten."

Both duelists stood fixed in place, waiting to see the hat start its drop to the cemetery ground. Egiap knew that now was the time for her intervention in the dueling process. She had her hand on the dagger and was about to hurl it at Barilleaux when a solitary figure atop one of the tallest tombs along the lighted avenue yelled out, "Vengeance is mine saith the Lord!" Everyone looked up at the figure outlined against the full moon. But one of the duelists acted on the moment as the ghostlike figure disappeared from the tomb skyline.

Barilleaux fired his pistol at Solomon and grazed him on the left arm. It burned a bit, but there was no flow of blood. A hole was there in the upper sleeve. Solomon now extended his right arm to take aim at Barilleaux.

"Don't shoot me now! Don't shoot!" shouted Barilleaux. "It is not fair. The duel has been interfered with and should end immediately! I did not mean to fire my pistol. That distraction caused me to pull the trigger."

"Mr. Witcher, it is your right and privilege to take your shot at your antagonist at this moment. It is your initiative," stated Bartholomew coldly and without judgment in his voice.

Now echoing through the cemetery tombs came the words again, "Vengeance is mine saith the Lord!" Egiap held up a dagger, his ivory-handle dagger, so Solomon could see it. Solomon discharged his weapon into the night sky.

"My honor is no longer tarnished by Mr. Barilleaux," stated Solomon in a benign voice. "But I must insist that Mr. Barilleaux remain after the duel officials depart."

"Mr. Barilleaux, you must remain," requested Bartholomew in a commanding voice.

"I desire to know what all of this means!" stated Barilleaux excitedly as all but Solomon, Egiap, and Barilleaux left the lighted area. Ann had previously put herself out of sight during the pace count for the duel. Zethro had not been in sight since he came running to say the group was arriving before the duel.

Now the flamebeaux were being extinguished one by one by Zethro. He left four burning in the middle of the area. There Barilleaux, Solomon, and Egiap gathered for discussion. Egiap knew that Zethro and Ann were both nearby in the shadows. The full moon still reigned in the nighttime sky. For a moment silence was the moon's king.

Then the cemetery took dominance with its eerie stillness and magical atmosphere. The people looked from the lighted area to the now fewer shadows lurking all around them. Barilleaux seemed tense now in the limited light and the silence. He saw Ann emerge from among the tombs. Then he saw Zethro follow her into the light.

"My little whore," he said to Ann, "jist why were yew here in this cemetery to witness this duel? And what is that dumb darkie Zethro doing here?"

Barilleaux, now feeling more adequate to the situation, began assuming his old mantle of arrogance and superiority. Egiap moved closer to Barilleaux and blew a powder from the palm of her left hand into his face. Almost immediately he collapsed into a weak fetal position on the cemetery ground.

Zethro moved to where Barilleaux had collapsed on the ground and picked him up to resettle him against one of the above-ground tombs. Zethro then extinguished three of the last four of the torches. The one left burning was directly in front of Barilleaux who was leaning against the tomb. Barilleaux moaned loudly and opened his eyes but did not move otherwise. Zethro and Ann assumed standing positions on each side of Barilleaux.

"Is that what you did to me across the river?" asked Solomon in disbelief at what he had just witnessed.

"No. Barilleaux merely can not move. He possesses command of all of his senses. He is motionless on his own. He understands what we say and can hear and see normally by now. He can not speak," answered Egiap.

Egiap drew the dagger from her cloak once again and offered it to Solomon.

"I thought you were going to kill him with my dagger," said Solomon.

"I thought so as well," said Egaip. "But he does not deserve that kind of death. He does not deserve a quick death. He will pay for what he has done to those less fortunate than he in a way more commensurate with his application of pain, suffering, and death."

"What do you mean?" asked Solomon as he took the dagger from her.

"He will be hexed here and now—to last the remainder of his life. God will determine how long he will be on this earth. I shall not make that determination." Egiap paused and drew a long breath. "Now I am only an instrument in the hands of the Almighty."

The single torch in the middle of the cemetery gave off an eerie illumination—something of the supernatural ilk, a foreboding and frightening feeling. The four people standing and the one recumbent seemed frozen in the hot, humid night. The full moon and the dim torch light did not shine on the lone figure in the shadows of one of the tombs. It was Xenophones, listening to the proceedings.

Egiap began reciting a litany of the half-truths, falsehoods, lies, and demonic deeds of James Barilleaux. She listed groups of persons and specific names of those that had their lives affected adversely by the man. At one point the four heard sobbing from somewhere to the left of them. Egiap paused until it ceased. She knew it was Xeno. She now knew her plan and ritual would definitely work.

"Each of you show me the red stone I had given you."

Zethro and Solomon each drew a red stone from their pockets and held it out for Egiap to see. Ann pulled the cork red pendant with the chain stretched for Egiap to see.

"Ann, did you place a red stone at the monument at the entrance?"

"Yus, I place it dere on de death head column," replied Ann.

"That is for the one who called me by name O'Suilleabhain on the streets of New Orleans. Each of you keep always the red stone."

Egiap looked at Barilleaux there against the tomb. "This small red stone is for him. I place it in his mouth for him to swallow into his bowels, to remain there for eternity. It will never dissolve, except in the fires of Hell." With those words she held up the smallest of the seven red stones given her and stepped over to Barilleaux. She opened his mouth and put the stone in his mouth, forcing him to swallow it. "Now you have eaten your sin, and it shall eat at you from your insides until you are taken from this life and delivered into the prepared afterlife for you in perdition."

Egiap turned to the others there with her. "You must go. I must conduct the remainder of the ritual with only Barilleaux and these dead here in the cemetery. Zethro and Ann, go wait at the monument at the entranceway of the cemetery. Go immediately and do not look back at me!"

Ann and Zethro, without hesitation, turned to walk to the entrance. They hurriedly walked without looking back or uttering a word. Solomon watched them disappear into the darkness of the cemetery.

Solomon turned back to look at Egiap. She was kneeling at the right side of Barilleaux. Solomon looked at Barilleaux's eyes. They were wild! They seemed on fire on the inside! "Do not gaze too long upon the man," came a warning from Egiap.

Solomon turned his attention back to Egiap. When she knelt next to Barilleaux, her dress hem and long cloak exposed her right ankle. In the flickering light of the single torch and the brightest light of the full moon thus far that night, he noticed something that seemed to be tied around Egiap's right ankle. He focused his sight and all of his attention on what appeared to be a red string. But suddenly Egiap rose and turned her attention to Solomon.

She said, "We must part now. I must complete the ritual alone with this man. He must feel my presence and the presence of those who died in the epidemic because of him. You have served well and even endured a minor wound. You have nothing more to do with this matter. Go about your business in New Orleans and do not seek me. I will not be found by you or others for a time."

"But, Egiap . . . "

"Do not be remorseful," she said as she smiled her mysterious smile at him and looked him in the eyes. "I have one other item for you, Solomon." She reached into her cloak and pulled out a red Irish linen gris-gris bag. "I placed the seventh red stone in the bag to accompany its other six mojo items. I believe the gris-gris bag will not be in your hands long."

"Thank you. Thank you," said Solomon with gratitude and disappointment in his voice. He took the gris-gris bag and put it in his pocket.

Egiap in a strong, decisive voice now spoke, "You must go! The red stone will serve as our connection. Let it remind you of me." She clasped his hands, pulled him close, stood on her tiptoes to kiss Solomon with a fierce passion, and bowed her head for a few moments. "You must depart this place!" she said as she let his hands go. She admonished, "Do not look back!"

Solomon turned and hurried away. He reached the entrance and saw Ann and Zethro waiting there as directed. Ann, as soon as she saw him, said, "Dat red stone I puts here be gone."

"It is?" replied Solomon. "What does that mean? Who found it?"

"It be dat street preacher. I be bettin'," advanced Ann.

"Do Mistress Egypt knows dat?" asked Zethro.

"It be part of her magicals," replied Ann. "Mistress Egypt know what dat she know."

Solomon asked, "Are the two of you going back into the cemetery?"

"No, sur, massa, nots me. I nots be in dere no times witout de Mistress," quickly said Zethro.

"No, we been tole to waits here, and dat's what we two do," added Ann. "Mistress Egypt be out here when she finish."

"I was directed to go about my business; so, that must be what I am to do. But do you know what will happen to Barilleaux?" asked Solomon.

"Dat man, he be wishin' he be ded insted of whats de Mistress puts in de future fer him. Dats all dat I kin say," replied Ann.

"What about Egiap? Where will she be? What did she mean that she could not be found?" asked Solomon.

"Da Mistress mean jist what dat she say. Her and us goes into hidin' from de world for some time. Only her knows de end of dat time," said Ann. "Me and Zethro jist goes to take care of de Mistress. Only her know where us'n goes and . . . "

"Where do you usually go when she retreats from the outside world?"

"Mistress Egypt forbid us to tole anybody. No more sayin' 'bout dat," Ann said quickly.

"At least tell me why she retreats," said Solomon, looking directly into Ann's eyes and focusing his powers of persuasion to obtain an answer.

202

"Yew be voodoo mon," said Ann. "Yew makes me talks too much."

"Tell me what I want to know," forcefully said Solomon to her. "Just tell me why, and I will leave you."

A strained and stressed look appeared on Ann's face. She tried to resist answering the question but could not do so. "Mistress Egypt get run-down when her hexes be used, and her must rest and gits her strength back. She drained of purpose and energy." Ann appeared to want to say something else but stopped short.

"And?"

"Please don'ts gits mad ats me, Mr. Voodoo Man," said Ann softly with a pitiful countenance on her face. "Me, I wants de best fer Mistress Egypt . . . "

"What are you trying to say to me?" demanded Solomon.

"I tole her dat yew not the red string man she search fer. But her, she tought dat yew be dat one she looked for rat here in de city. She say it ain't true, but me, I can tell dat she in love with yew. But me, I be de one to tell hur dat yew not have dat red string on yore ankle when we ober dere 'cross de river, so yew be not de man she hoped. I be de one to hurt her. When Mistress Egypt hurt, she retreats to a place within hurself to recover. But she had to deals with Barilleaux afore she halted her work. She done use yew to hep her wit de justice on Barilleaux. Don'ts hurts me for me tellin' de truth." Crying, Ann motioned to Zethro. He came over to stand by her.

"I am not angry with any of you, especially Mistress Egypt."

Solomon paused a moment, looking at the two of them. He smiled, turned, and walked down the city street. He was dejected; he was sorrowful; he was overwhelmed with a feeling of remorse and sadness. Now he hurried to get away from the cemetery. He thrust both of his hands deep into his trouser pockets. He felt one of his derringers in one pocket. In the other pocket his fingers reached deep and felt a loose thread. It reminded him of the red string he had lost.

Feeling a deep disappointment and a bit of depression, Solomon continued his walk back to the boarding house. He slept long and hard and did not awaken until the early afternoon. He would be leaving New Orleans in two days. He would try to get a chair at the poker gathering once more to win traveling money. He would make two stops this afternoon—one at the coffee house and one at THE MUSTARD SEED. He set out first for the coffee house.

He entered the establishment and greeted Babineaux. There was a chair available, and Solomon paid his admission ante. He conversed with the bartender for a short time, inquiring of Ramley, Sisera, and Bartholomew, while sipping a drink for a time.

He left that establishment with a spring in his gait. He was now ready to turn over the gris-gris bag to that old woman in THE MUSTARD SEED. He felt the bag in his vest pocket. He had not looked at the contents of the bag. He feared contradicting its mojo or whatever power it possessed. He turned on the street that the old woman and her shop were on. He walked a bit faster, passing some other pedestrians. He now looked for the sign and the window filled with a hodge-podge of goods. He spied the entranceway to the shop, but he stopped dead in his tracks at the front door. He was stunned at what he saw.

The shop looked as if it had been vacant for a week or two. A board was loosely nailed across the door. There were no goods displayed in the window, and the sign THE MUSTARD SEED was covered with dust and spider webs. On the walkway he asked several passers-by about the shop and the old woman. The first three ignored him and continued on their way. But an elderly black man sitting in a rocking chair on the wooden walkway noticed Solomon and his questions about the shop and said something that Solomon did not understand in the din of the street traffic and the noise of the pedestrians. Solomon walked over to the man and asked him to repeat what he had said. "She be dead. Missus Maxzille jist up and died in dere one day some mornings ago. She be dead. Hur shop be cleaned out." The black man continued, "I sits out here ebery day, and I ain't seen nobody in or out of dere since de day it be cleaned out. Dat day a man nailed de board 'cross de door." Solomon stood there, staring back at the door and the sign.

Solomon felt the gris-gris bag in his vest pocket and pulled it out to look it over. He thought that he must look inside the shop; in fact, he felt something urging him to go inside to look around. He thanked the old black man and walked back to the front of the shop. He reached for the loosely nailed board across the wooden door. He pulled it, and it almost fell to the threshold by itself. He propped it against the wall by the threshold. He pushed the door, and it creaked open.

The air was musty. His eyes surveyed the room. Empty shelves and empty tables full of cobwebs and dirt and dust stood silent. He took a few steps, going farther into the room. He remembered the back corner where the old Oriental woman sat in her rocking chair. He moved over to the old rickety chair and thought he smelled a faint minty odor. The rocking chair was covered with cobwebs and dust. He noticed a spider crawling slowly on the top of the back of the old woman's chair. Then the spider began climbing a partially unseen spider web upward toward one of the empty shelves that it had connected with its silken web. He watched it slowly ascending to the dusty shelf. He noted as well a large fly caught in the web; it was wriggling, trying to loosen its restraints. Solomon now thought about what he was to do with the gris-gris bag. He remembered the old woman spoke of consequences. He thought what she said had truth to it because of the red string on Egiap's ankle and that red string the old woman had him to tie about his ankle. He stood there watching the captured insect and imagined that he was captured in the same way. But the spider's renewed rapid movement up the web to the shelf drew his attention now. He followed the spider with his eyes. There on the shelf he spied a piece of bright red string. It had no dust or cobwebs on it. It looked to be placed there just a few hours ago. The door was still open, and sunlight flooded in. Solomon could see no footprints in the dirt and dust on the floor except his.

Solomon picked up the red string, thought for a moment, and then tied it around his right ankle. He took two quick breaths and then one long, deep inhale. He let it out as he placed the red Irish linen gris-gris bag on the shelf, replacing the piece of red string. He thought he smelled that minty aroma in the air again. That brought a smile to his face. He glanced back at the old rocking chair and imagined the old woman sitting there. "Here is your gris-gris bag, Maxzille. I hope I am not too late with it." He turned and walked out the door. Outside, he picked up the old board and put it across the door in the same nail holes. He used his unloaded derringer to hit on the old nails. The board stayed in place.

Solomon walked back to the boarding house and rested for the gathering card game that night. Being his punctual self, he ambled into the coffee house a few minutes after nine that evening. Babineaux was there behind the bar and waved, and Sisera saw him from across the crowded bar room, smiled really big, and weaved among the tables and chairs to get to him as quickly as she could. Sisera took his arm and walked him up the stairs.

Sisera looked up at Solomon as they climbed the stairs slowly and said, "Mr. Witcher, will theah ever be a time that y'all kin spend some time with me?" She smiled seductively at Solomon and pushed herself more against him. They proceeded along the balcony toward Ramley and the double doors to the gathering room.

Solomon, just before acknowledging and speaking to Ramley, looked at Sisera and whispered so only she could hear, "Will you be here all night?" Then he separated from her grasp and greeted Ramley, who opened the doors for the both of them. They continued to walk and went to the middle of the gathering room.

"I will wait for you," said Sisera as she turned to leave.

Solomon got into the game in a few minutes after he talked with Bartholomew and exchanged money for poker chips. As Solomon was taking his seat at the table, Bartholomew, smiling, said to him, "No arguments about honor tonight, Mr. Witcher?"

"I think not. I do not see any adversaries at the table, other than for the poker hands."

Bartholomew added, "Word is that Mr. Barilleaux, while not injured by a dueling pistol, has taken ill in an odd sort of manner."

"What is his problem?" asked Solomon before taking his chair at the table. He stood there in place to listen to Bartholomew. The others kept playing the hand they were in. When one of them reached to pull in the pot for his winning hand, the others all looked at Bartholomew as he talked.

Bartholomew now said, "Mr. Barilleaux seems, according to what we heard on the street, to now be afflicted with ailments of the brain and the bowels. People are saying that he complains of daytime abdominal pains akin to his bowels and stomach being eaten from the inside like thousands of maggots gorging themselves on his innards; and then when he sleeps at night, he sleeps fitfully and intermittently with dreams of his being in the center of the Girod Street Cemetery surrounded by thousands of dead souls in their reanimated corpses consumed by Yellow Jack, screaming his name and clawing and biting his body. It is said that never a single moment day or night is he not affected by his illness. His doctors are attempting to help him with his situation, but nothing they have done has alleviated any of his suffering. It is said that he may have to endure this, this ailment, this curse that has befallen him as long as he lives."

Solomon now said, "Mr. Barilleaux was quite all right when I last saw him at the cemetery. In fact, the last words I heard him say reflected his arrogant attitude, and the last time I looked at him, he was in no pain at all."

Bartholomew replied, "Only God Almighty knows the man's affliction. Let's hope none of us ever acquire what that man did."

"Shall we continue with the next deal, my friends?" asked Solomon.

The cards were dealt, and the game continued until after midnight. At the break, Sisera came into the room with several other pretty young women. She clung to Solomon the entire break time. After the game ended and all the players were leaving, she awaited Solomon outside the double doors. Solomon tipped Bartholomew and Ramley as he left the room with Sisera on his arm. They did not go downstairs but turned into an open doorway in one of the balcony rooms on the way to the stairs. Sisera closed the door and smiled at Solomon.

The next morning Solomon awoke before Sisera did, washed, and dressed in preparation for going to his bank to conduct some last business before leaving early the next morning. Sisera had drunk much more than did Solomon; so, he thought he would allow her to sleep longer. Before he left the room, he went over to the bed, kissed her on her lips, rousing her only a little, and placed a wad of bills in her hand. He said softly to her as he unclasped her hand full of money, "I hope you are here when I return."

Solomon attended to his business that day and settled with Mrs. Ducote that evening after supper. The next morning he ate his last breakfast cooked by Mrs. Ducote, went back to the room to gather his belongings, and bid her good-bye. Her last words to him rang in his ears, "I hope the fortune you seek is that of love."

In less than an hour Solomon boarded his ship bound for New York. As the ship was leaving the dock, Solomon, who was on the upper deck looking ashore at the buildings, heard over the noise the loud "cawing" of a crow. He saw it fly toward his ship and then veer off to his right, the direction the ship was moving. In the distance he saw an isolated figure in a gray cloak with a black hood. "Egiap," he murmured in a low voice. He felt his heart pound. The lone figure turned and walked away from the river.

To Be Continued . . .

CPSIA information can be obtained
at www.ICGtesting.com
Printed in the USA
LVHW080536140519
617763LV00023B/406/P